MY NEXT DATE

RAISED BY WOLVES BOOK 2

CASEY MORALES

WWW.AUTHORCASEYMORALES.COM

A NOTE OF CAUTION

The following story is best categorized as an MM Romance in which the main plot depicts gay men and their romantic entanglements. There are scenes describing sexual acts, some of which are explicit and may be inappropriate for those below a certain age.

JOIN OUR COMMUNITY

Before you get lost in Michael's journey again, take a moment to join our community. You'll receive updates, advanced notice of new releases, discounts, and freebies. It'll be fun.

Click Here to Learn More

PREFACE

I can't remember ever dreaming of having my wrists tied to bedposts with silk ties. It wasn't that long ago I'd thought all gays lived in New York or California. Who knew they were everywhere, and quite willing to offer their neckwear in service to the greater good? At least, to *my* greater good.

Ah, the memories.

The bed with the silk isn't where our story begins. It's just a scene from the past I can't get out of my head. You know, that memory of heart-pounding fear and adrenaline combined with the tingle of warm oil drizzling across skin? The sweet hint of cologne mingled with a day's sweat?

Sorry, I got lost.

Just hang with me.

It'll be worth it.

1

———————

I was completely intimidated the first time my roommate, Peter, bugged me about joining the gym where he worked out. He was a Greek god, an actual model who looked like one of those unreal men on the cover of the magazines I *definitely* never looked at every time I passed them in the grocery store. Peter worked out twice a day and coached other people in their workouts for another three or four hours. I hadn't ever met anyone with a body like his, and it was such a waste, especially since we lived together, because he was straight.

Never mind that I thought I was straight too. Yes, I know. I'd had hot man-sex twice and couldn't get the images of Joseph out of my mind, especially as I lay awake at night wishing his warmth was beside me, but I *wanted* to be straight.

So I was. For the moment. I thought.

Sigh.

The third or fourth—or tenth—time Peter asked me to go to the gym and start working out, I gave in. I was *that* skinny kid. You know, the one who could never gain weight. My mom cooked buttery fried goodness most nights, and we drank sweet tea so thick it could give you a cavity just looking at it. It didn't matter. I could eat anything and never gain a pound.

As strange as that might seem to those who struggle with losing weight, I was insecure about my bean-pole-ness and intimidated by all the perfect people I imagined seeing lifting small houses at the gym. Peter said I should be thankful. He said I had "the perfect body type" for adding muscle, and he was sure he could turn me into something hot if I just put in the work.

It sounded like a *lot* of work to me.

I tossed my fear and childhood insecurities aside and followed muscle-god roomie like a lost puppy to the gym. It was pretty much what I expected—men with necks bigger than their heads lifting small houses. They tended to congregate in the section with warnings about not lifting too much without a partner. They weren't just big. They were huge.

Oddly, they were very nice. Every single Popeye acknowledged me with a smile or nod, as if greeting a new brother into their fraternity. I hadn't expected that.

By the third or fourth week, when it became obvious I wasn't going to be one of those guys who paid for the membership and never returned, the muscle gods learned my name and greeted me warmly. They offered to spot me and gave me a high-five when I did something particularly painful. It was nice, in a really masochistic way.

One afternoon, I was straining with all my spindly might and noticed a guy I hadn't seen before. He was running on a treadmill. I blinked through sweat and focused. Blondish-brown hair bounced as he ran, though a few locks stuck to his forehead. He wore a thirsty white tank top that drank every drop of sweat it touched and clung to a ridiculous set of abs.

His shoulders glistened as they bobbed. Every time he smiled at a different person who called out his name, his brilliant white teeth lit up that corner of the gym.

Okay, maybe it wasn't that dramatic, but you get the picture.

Despite his obvious sweat-soaked hotness, Mr. Sweaty Runner caught my eye because every few minutes, a different club member would wander up to him and shake his hand or wave or call out in greeting. Nashville was a town where half the people you met were either students or aspiring musicians. I'd become numb to that scene, and barely kept up with who was famous and who wasn't. I had no clue who this very popular hottie was.

Peter smacked the back of my head playfully, pulling me back to our side of the gym.

"Enough rest. You've been sitting there for at least five minutes. Let's go."

I wanted to toss the weights at him, but that would've required lifting them and he would've won, so I asked about hottie instead. "Is that guy up there famous or something? Everybody seems to know him."

Peter grunted. "Yeah, he's a singer, or wants to be. Nice enough guy. Welcome to Nashville."

With that, Peter grabbed my wrists and hoisted them to the bar dangling over my head, giving me no choice but to resume the lat-straining-torture-thing.

Don't hurt yourself on all my technical terms. I try to be precise.

A WEEK PASSED, AND I SAW SINGER BOY AT THE GYM NEARLY every day, his flock of women—and men—trailing him from treadmill to bicep curl, trying to look like they weren't following his every move. It was pretty funny to watch. When one of his loyal geese would catch me watching, their head would whip in the other direction, and they'd magically find the need to work a random body part not on that day's rotation.

Singer Boy never seemed to notice. He just kept working out and flashing his pearly whites.

Peter and I got to the gym late Friday afternoon. Singer Boy had already showered and changed into tight, faded jeans and a clingy black T-shirt. The black made his green eyes leap out. Holy cow, they were *really* green.

Anyway.

I had just finished a set on the leg-press-device-of-death when someone walked up to Peter. I was facing the wall and couldn't see who it was.

"Hey, Peter. I've got a gig tonight at Rowdie's. A big producer promised he'd be there, so I really need a good crowd. Can I count you in?"

There was a crinkling of paper, probably a flyer.

"I'll try," Peter said in a tone I knew meant he wouldn't go anywhere near Rowdie's.

"Thanks. This could be my big break if it works out. It's been a long time coming."

"Good luck," Peter said, followed by the distinct sound of paper being stuffed into a pocket. He turned back to me. "Again. Two more sets."

I hated Peter sometimes.

An hour later, I staggered into our apartment, thighs ablaze with leg-day pain, and threw myself onto the couch. Peter trotted in without the slightest hint of soreness.

Again with the hating Peter thing.

He tossed his keys on the counter, then emptied his pockets. I looked up.

"What's that?" I asked, indicating the wadded-up paper he'd dropped by his keys.

He hurled the wad into my head. "That wannabe-famous guy at the gym is playing some bar tonight. He says there's a producer going, and it might be his big break. Same story, different night."

That got my attention. "Are you going?"

He laughed. "Nope. I hate bars. Go if you want to. I don't think he cares who's there, just that there's a crowd."

I stared blankly. I'd never been to a bar. Weren't they the den of evil and the birthplace of sin? People drank alcohol there. I'd never had alcohol either.

Did you forget already? I was raised by wolves.

"That's OK. Bars aren't my thing either," I said weakly, wanting desperately to see Singer Boy in his element and find out if bars were really as vile as I had been taught.

"Whatever. I'm meeting Jen for a late bite. We might grab a movie after. See you later."

Jen was Peter's on-and-off girlfriend. At the moment, she was on.

As soon as the door slammed shut and Peter's footfalls faded into the night, I smoothed the flyer against my leg and held it up. Singer Boy's set started in an hour.

I had to move.

I walked into Rowdie's and blinked a few times so my eyes could adjust to the dim light. The aroma of cigarettes tickled my nose. There were ten, maybe fifteen round high-top tables scattered about, with a brightly lit, makeshift stage holding court from one end of the room. From the flyer and Singer Boy's perma-smile at the gym, I had expected the place to be packed. I was the fifth person to enter. Only seven total would show up. So much for a roaring crowd.

I looked nervously around and picked a table near the back, as far from the stage and other people as I could get. A perky waitress wandered by and giggled when I ordered a Coke. Was that not OK in a bar?

A moment later, Coke in hand, my eyes darted from stage to bar, taking in every detail. This den of ill repute seemed awfully tame. People weren't humping or fighting. They were just sitting and drinking, some eating, enjoying themselves. Interesting.

"Mind if I sit with you?" A voice startled me.

I looked up to find a man with short dark hair and kind eyes blinking at me. His short crop revealed a faint dusting of gray that intruded around his temples.

"I'm Dwayne," he said, extending a hand. Were we supposed to shake hands in a bar? Was this a business thing? I shook it, and he sat without waiting for permission. "Thanks. I hate sitting up front at these things. How do you know Jason?"

For the second time, I was startled. "Jason?"

"The singer. He's supposed to start any minute, but he's always late." He chuckled.

Singer Boy's name was Jason. Check.

"Oh, I don't really know him. We work out at the same gym. He was making the rounds today, handing out these flyers, and I thought I'd check it out." I tried to sound disinterested and casual.

Dwayne looked down at the flyer I had tossed on the table and smiled. "I helped him make those. He's definitely *not* shy."

Before I could answer, Jason raced up to our table and wrapped Dwayne in a big hug. "Thank you for coming. I'm so nervous." His head swiveled as he scanned the room. "Mr. Best isn't here yet, but he promised he'd come. Dwayne, this could be the night."

He sounded giddy. I guess that was to be expected. Back then, there was no *American Idol* or *The Voice*, or any other competition show that vaulted unknown artists into stardom. To be discovered, you had to actually *be discovered*. It was nearly impossible. If I had been a singer with a shot at a producer, I would've been giddy too.

Dwayne finally turned and introduced me. I reminded Jason about the gym, and he nodded as if he actually remembered seeing me among his throng. He clearly didn't. Then he vanished to prepare for his time on stage.

I caught Dwane watching the interaction with more than passing interest. I guess my stare lingered on Jason's jeans a little too long as he walked away, because he said, "You *like* him?"

Startle number three.

"Uh, I guess. I mean, um, I don't know him or anything. He seems like a nice guy." I was articulate.

Dwayne chuckled and peered over his glass of Jack and Coke. A second glass filled with limes sat next to it. He would squeeze a lime into his drink after every sip; there had to be as much lime in there as there was Coke. Was this normal bar behavior? No one else seemed to be doing it. Weird.

Thankfully, the stage lights flashed as Jason stepped up to the mic, saving me from further examination. I got the feeling Dwayne didn't miss much.

Jason sounded good. I mean, really good.

He played guitar and sang songs he'd written himself. When Dwayne told me he would perform his own work, I'd groaned inwardly, expecting a long evening of bad music. But this guy had talent. He sang about love and loss, and lost love, and love he wished he hadn't lost, and love he was glad he lost —then a song about a lake in a town where he met someone he loved and lost.

My keen sense of observation picked up a theme, but it still sounded good.

The more I watched and listened, the better he looked.

What was it about performers, especially singers, that made them so much more alluring the minute they stepped behind a microphone? Jason didn't get all dressed up or wear makeup or anything, but on that stage, under the annoyingly bright lights zip-tied to the bar's ceiling, he looked even better than he had in the gym that first day. Now that his hair wasn't a sweaty, matted mess, I could see how it curled slightly at the ends and waved in the air from the vent above the stage. It wasn't quite Marilyn and her white dress, but it was nice.

He was dreamy, and he was singing.

A couple times he actually looked over at our table and flashed that broad, incredibly warm smile I'd seen him give others a hundred times at the gym. I tried not to swoon, then realized he was smiling at Dwayne, acknowledging his friend and some secret meaning hidden within the tune.

For his part, Dwayne barely spoke throughout the evening, but I caught him watching me a few times, a catlike grin playing across his weathered face.

When Jason wrapped and the stage finally fell quiet, the lights in the bar gradually brightened. Dwayne stifled a yawn into his elbow and looked up. "What did you think?"

"He's great. I'm surprised he hasn't got a record deal yet," I said.

Dwayne laughed sardonically. "That's *the dream*, but he's been doing this for years. I think if it was going to happen, it would've by now."

"What about the producer tonight?"

He shook his head. "Never showed. Again, that happens all the time. They promise, get the performer all excited, then stand them up. It's sad, really."

"Huh." I'd never known anyone trying to make it in music. This was news to me.

Dwayne yawned again. "There's a group of us going out after this. You should join us."

It was already eleven o'clock. Where could anyone possibly go at that hour on a Friday night? I was baffled.

It must've shown on my face because Dwayne chuckled. His eyes held that amused, knowing gaze of one who'd discovered a baby learning to walk—or at least realizing that walking was a thing. I hadn't even tried to stand yet, much less walk.

"It's just a few of us going to celebrate with Jason on his big performance. We were going to celebrate the producer, but he's still AWOL. Come have a drink."

"Alright. I guess." I didn't even think to ask where we were going. If it was to have a drink, I assumed another bar.

My first night was turning into a two-fer. Look at me, becoming a Coke-drinking barfly stud.

Jason stopped by and gave Dwayne another hug. He sure hugged a lot. He acknowledged me with a quick smile and thanked me for coming. I don't think he remembered my name or how we knew each other—again. So much for validation.

I climbed into Betty, my cooler-than-cool Saturn sedan, and followed Dwayne's eight-hundred-year-old Toyota something-or-other. It was small, zippy, and thoroughly covered in rust—but who was I to judge? It was easy to follow because nothing else looked like it.

We drove for twenty minutes before I realized I was thoroughly lost. I'd never been in this part of town before. It was one of those industrial parks with long, low, sprawling buildings. From an airplane's view, they almost looked like bugs, with all the trailers pulled up to the loading docks serving as legs. Were we going to a warehouse? Who'd put a bar all the way out here?

We finally pulled into a massive parking lot. There were hundreds of cars already cooling. I looked for signage or anything that might tell me where we were, but there was nothing. The building before us was as nondescript as every other factory or warehouse around, save for the line of a dozen people waiting to enter.

I parked and found Dwayne waiting for me near the entrance.

"Ready? The others already went inside. We'll meet up in the country bar."

"Country bar?" I asked.

He nodded. "This is more of a complex than a bar. You'll see."

We waited our turn. I tried not to wince as the doorman held out a palm and said, "Welcome to the Connection. Five bucks."

Ever-observant Dwayne noticed and waved me off, paying my fee. "My invite, my treat."

That was nice.

As we entered, my head spun. We walked through giant double doors into a wide hallway that could squeeze a dozen people shoulder to shoulder without touching the sides. It was packed. We could barely move, and the mass of quickly heating bodies was inching forward. A thunderous rhythm pulsed from somewhere ahead, and I could make out flashes of light through an opening thirty or so yards away.

We got about halfway down the hallway when Dwayne grabbed my arm and pulled me through an opening on the left side. The booming bass was replaced by a happy, twangy tune better played in a Western movie than a bar in the industrial heart of Nashville. The crowd thinned, and tight-fitting T-shirts and tank tops were replaced by gaudy buckles and fringy tops with silver buttons. Walking through that opening, we literally set foot onto a different planet, one filled with country music and very country patrons.

"What do you want to drink?" Dwayne's voice snapped me back to him.

"Coke, thanks."

He shook his head and chuckled. "Come help me. I'll need an extra hand."

I followed and waited with him in the queue that was only a few men deep. As we stood there, something struck, and I turned to Dwayne. "Where are all the women?"

He looked up at me with a furrowed brow. "What?"

"The women. I don't see any in here. Looks like some of the guys had to dance with each other because there aren't any girls here yet."

In that moment, Dwayne gave me a look I'll never forget. His eyes flew wide, and his mouth twitched between a smile and a frozen 'O' shape, as if he couldn't decide—or believe— what was standing in front of him. Maybe it was what I asked, or maybe I had something in my teeth. I'd never seen anyone look so utterly baffled.

Then he doubled over and gripped his sides.

When he righted himself, tears were streaming down his cheeks. He saw me gaping, and his laughter grew into near hyperventilation. Some of the guys standing around us turned to see what was so funny. I shrugged, dumbfounded.

By the time he managed to suck in enough air to breathe again, we stood before a bemused bartender wearing a foot-tall cowboy hat and leather vest. He'd forgotten his shirt; a furry, muscular chest poked through.

Dwayne turned to me and wiped his eyes. "You're going to need a real drink tonight. Trust me, Coke isn't going to cut it."

2

<hr>

I helped Dwayne carry the two glasses filled with limes and three brimming with Jack and Coke to a table on the outside patio. The night was cool and comfortable, and the patio was much quieter than anywhere we'd been in the Connection so far. It was a relief to sit and have a little personal space again.

Dwayne hadn't stopped chuckling to himself. He'd said something to the bartender, whom he obviously knew well, and Cowboy Rick nearly peed himself before pouring our drinks.

I wasn't sure I was ready to know the joke, but curiosity got the best of me. "Care to share what's so funny?"

He looked up, eyes twinkling. "Why don't you take a good sip of that drink first?"

I'd only ever tasted wine once. It had been five years ago in Australia. I was there at the National Scout Jamboree representing the United States, along with two thousand other Boy Scouts.

Don't laugh. It was a really cool trip.

Anyway, the French scouts, Fleur-de-something, had homemade wine and were passing out samples. I hadn't even noticed when my best friend handed me a cup and I took a sip. I gagged so hard I thought I'd spew all over France. It was awful and tasted like a soured version of whatever drink it used to be.

Yes, I know, that was the point. At the time, I didn't even know I was drinking wine, much less what to expect. It was vile.

And here I sat, with a man twice my age in a bar without women—with men dancing together to country music—about to drink hard liquor. The two-fer just became a hat trick.

Yes, hockey reference. Just roll with it.

I lifted the glass and looked at it with deep suspicion, as if a snake might leap out from behind the ice cubes and snap at my nose. I didn't mean to give Dwayne puppy-dog eyes, but when I looked up, there was a mix of amusement and pity in his gaze.

"Michael, this is a gay bar."

I downed half my drink in one swallow.

"Whoa. Easy. They make them strong here," he said with genuine concern.

I finished the drink and looked up. "*Gay* bar?"

Before tonight, I'd never been to a bar of any kind. I didn't know the gays had their own bars.

He nodded silently and watched as the color drained from my face.

A moment later, he asked, "You didn't know we were coming to a gay bar?"

I didn't trust my voice, so I just shook my head and tried

not to make eye contact with the guy at the next table who kept staring at me.

"I need another drink." I stood before Dwayne could say anything. Thankfully, there was only one person ahead of me at the bar. I had time to gather my wits, but not long enough to be alone in a gay bar without my life raft, if that's what Dwayne was.

"You came. Dwayne said you might."

I turned and was shocked to see Jason leaning against the bar. He'd changed from the outfit he'd worn on stage into a tight white T-shirt with the name of some band I didn't recognize scrawled in script across his chest. I could see the definition of his pecs through the lettering.

"Uh. Yeah. I'm here," I spluttered. "Um. You sounded good tonight."

"Thanks. Stupid producer stood me up, but I'm used to that now." He waved at the bartender, who leaned over and kissed him. He *kissed* him—on the mouth, in front of me; in front of everyone.

My jaw must've still been on the floor when Jason turned around because he started chuckling. "You OK?"

I nodded fervently. I wasn't OK.

I could see his wheels turning, then click into place. He leaned over and half-whispered a question I'd never forget. No one had ever asked me that before. "You like boys, don't you?"

The music faded away. All the men and lights and drinks and smoke—it all vanished. Jason was the only person in the world, and I felt like I was falling. Not falling for him, *actually* falling. My head spun, and I lost track of where I was.

When the warmth of his hand on my arm brought me back

to the present, I managed a weak smile. "Sure. I like boys fine."

He cocked his head again, smiled, then vanished into the sea of men.

I blinked a few times as Cowboy Rick plopped another Jack and Coke in front of me. He batted his eyes and gave me a flirty smile as I handed him the last of the paper money in my pocket. I didn't know whether he was actually flirting or angling for a better tip, but he laughed as he walked away. I'm guessing the bar lighting hadn't hidden my blush.

I escaped back to the quiet of the patio to find Dwayne deep in conversation with two other men now seated around the table. They were older—and by that, I mean in their thirties, not *nearly* as old as Dwayne's ancient forties—and both leaning forward on conspiratorial elbows. All three had that same catlike smile that lingered a moment too long when they noticed I'd returned.

"You made it back," Dwayne said. The other kitties grinned. One of them, the prettier one with hair a bit too tall for his face, looked me up and down like he was sizing me for a tuxedo. What was that all about?

Felines One and Two excused themselves, but Pretty Cat made a point of squeezing my shoulder as he walked by. Dwayne's eyes twinkled as he watched the exchange. Had there been an exchange? I didn't even know where we were, much less what was going on with the shoulder-squeezing, puffy-haired puddy tat.

"I ran into Jason at the bar," I said.

Dwayne brightened. "Oh? Is he coming out here?"

"No. He disappeared into the crowd. I think he's headed toward all the music." I paused and stared at my drink.

That moment has lingered in my memory for years. It's one of those still-frame moments when you later realize you'd been standing before the proverbial fork in life's road, but at the time, you had no idea what that tingly feeling in your neck was. My neck was definitely tingling its ass off. Wait, necks don't have asses, do they?

Anyway.

"He asked me the weirdest question," I said, then took a sip.

"Oh?" Dwayne arched a wiry, unkempt brow. He was very un-gay in that regard.

"Yeah. I guess he thought I looked uncomfortable or something. He asked if I liked boys."

Dwayne nearly spat out his drink, but stifled whatever laughter had tried to escape. A second and a swallow later, he looked up. "What did you say?"

"I told him I liked them fine. It just seemed like such a strange thing to ask."

Something clicked. I saw it in Dwayne's eyes.

He realized I was still clueless—that lone wolf cub lost in the woods with bears and otters and every other kind of animal wandering around me. His expression changed from amused observer to something akin to Yoda when he gave Luke Skywalker his first lesson. "Gay you are, asking he was."

OK, he didn't say it like that, but that's the gist. Yoda would've said it better.

I was shocked. *Gay? Me?* I could barely bring myself to *say* the G word. I sucked down my second Jack and Coke and never felt a thing.

"Are you OK?" Dwayne asked.

"Yeah, I am. I mean, I'm not. Yes, I'm fine, but no, I'm *not* gay." Articulate as ever though.

He nodded sagely. "OK. You seem to be handling this place alright. Did you not realize we were coming to a gay bar?"

I shook my head. "I'd never been to *any* bar before tonight, much less a gay one."

His eyes widened as if seeing some exotic animal at the zoo for the first time.

The lights flashed twice and I looked up, unsure if there was a fire or air raid or what.

"The show's starting. That's the two-minute warning," he said as he rose. "Come on. This should be fun."

There was that twinkle again, the one I now understood hid Dwayne's utter glee at exposing me to something else I'd never experienced.

This was going to be a long night.

3

<hr>

The herd was definitely moving with purpose. We made it out of the country bar with little trouble, but had to inch our way from there. I'd never seen so many people packed into one place—and the place was huge.

The hallway was crammed with new arrivals who'd skipped line dancing and were headed directly into the main part of the warehouse. It was around midnight, which was apparently when all gays instinctively knew they should arrive. I managed a look back and could see that the line out the glass double doors now wound through the parking lot, so far that I couldn't see its end. Dwayne had said they crammed two to three thousand people into this place every Friday and Saturday night, but seeing the throng of men in their painted-on T-shirts and jeans that nearly revealed which religion they followed—well, I was overwhelmed.

Shoulders bumped and brushed from all sides. The crowd crawled. The doormen didn't seem to care and kept letting more join the flow. They pressed tighter together as we shuffled forward.

I couldn't breathe. I started to sweat.

My eyes darted around, taking in the sea of men. Some locked eyes and smiled in a way that I was sure meant something, I just couldn't imagine what. I looked away as fast as my head would swivel.

And then it happened. My life raft floated away.

I'd lost Dwayne.

The hallway opened into a vast open space half a football field long. Lights flashed. Fast-paced music, heavily anchored with bass, throbbed through my body. Despite the strobing lights, the massive room was dark, and I couldn't make out faces well, only writhing shapes.

A different song began to play, this one with words everyone in the bar seemed to recognize, and a cheer rose with every arm as the dance floor hopped as a single beast.

Long bars on every wall served a constant stream of men. At the center of the room, a towering pillar rose to support the ceiling. Around the base of the pillar was a circular stage, on which shirtless men swayed and wiggled and strutted—*and rutted*—to the beat.

I panicked and found the darkest, emptiest corner I could find. There was no escaping the crowd, but it did thin out a bit around the edges. Leaning my back against the wall gave me some sense of security. At least a gay couldn't sneak up on me from behind.

Yes, I now know that's one of the main goals of the place. I didn't back then.

The lights rotated and flashed, and I looked up. I hadn't noticed the upper level before. This place went on forever.

A balcony encircled the entire dance floor area, but it

wasn't just a *look-over-the-edge* kind of balcony. It was wide enough to fit hundreds, and there were three bars on three of the walls. There was even a seating area with couches and puffy chairs at one end. Men were lined along the silver railing, drinks in hand, watching those below.

There was barely an inch of empty space in the whole place—and more men poured in with each passing moment.

Where did all these gay men come from? Had I died and gone to California?

My mind raced as a handsome guy with floppy hair passed by. Our eyes locked for only a second, but that was enough to make the temperature in the room skyrocket. I knew I should just make my way back to the exit, run to Betty, and flee to the safety of my apartment, but I couldn't move.

Couldn't? Wouldn't? I didn't know. I still don't.

Instinctively, I pressed my back to the wall. Good, it was actually a corner. No gay-sneak could get my side *or* my back. Secure in my hiding place, I did the only thing I could do. I watched.

I liked watching people. People were interesting. And this place was a petri dish of interesting.

When my nerves calmed enough for my semi-rational mind to take over, I was again stunned by what I saw. As the child of a very conservative preacher, I'd been taught that all gays were either child molesters or drag queens. It seemed strange. How could a man wanting to get into another man's pants automatically make him one of those two things? But who was I to challenge the wisdom of my father's religious teaching?

As I scanned the crowd, I didn't see anyone who looked

like a child molester. In fact, most of the men dancing and drinking looked to be in their twenties or thirties. Weren't most child molesters older than that? All I knew was, I didn't see any obvious ice-cream-truck drivers.

And I didn't see a single man in drag. I'd actually never seen one before, but was sure I'd know one when I saw it.

Everyone looked so normal. They looked happy and relaxed.

They looked like *me*.

Wait. How was that possible? These were *gays*! They weren't supposed to be normal or, I don't know, *anything* like me, but that's what hit me harder than a Jack and Coke with a whole glass's worth of lime.

Here I was, surrounded by more gay men than I knew existed outside their protective borders, and they looked like any other guys you might see in the real world. I mean, this *was* the real world, but it wasn't. This was a giant gay bubble. Right?

A gaggle of gays passed by, clearly headed somewhere in a hurry. They were all laughing hysterically. One of them came up for air and I overheard him say, "Come on, we're missing the show."

Right. Dwayne was headed to a show. Curiosity overcame fear and I followed the giggling gaggle.

They weaved through the crowd with practiced ease, carefully pressing palms against shoulders to move the men blocking their progress. I was the guy with the ball following his blockers. I just wished they'd told me what the goal line looked like before we crossed it.

As we entered another short hallway, the throbbing of

lights and music faded and was replaced by the sounds of something decidedly *showier*. The song had more words, was easier to recognize, and there was a performance quality to it that was very different from the mindless rhythm of the dance floor.

Ten yards later, my blockers skipped merrily into another massive room. Like the chamber of dance, there was a balcony on one end that held a bar and room for fifty or so. The main floor was a field of four-top tables crammed with laughing, drinking men. At the end, opposite the balcony, rose a stage roughly four feet above the floor spanning nearly the entire thirty-yard stretch of wall. A catwalk (is that what it's called?) stretched from the center of the stage halfway through the room.

I stopped walking and gaped as the performer I'd barely noticed marched down the catwalk like she owned the whole club. She was the only woman I'd seen in the bar so far, and was by far the tallest woman I'd ever seen in real life. Her dusty blue wig towered higher than Marge Simpson on a bad hair day. I knew performers wore crazy outfits, but I couldn't understand why this one had chosen a bedazzled version of Mr. Hefner's bunny costume, complete with floppy ears that protruded out the top of the mile-high hairdo.

And then I saw her boobs. Man, they were big. No, enormous. And they jiggled like Jell-O that needed more stiffener, or whatever that powder was called. I couldn't stop staring. How were those things real? Did the poor gal have back problems? My mind raced with questions.

Then someone in the crowd behind me said something about "him" lip-synching well. *Him*? What him? I looked around the stage and couldn't find anyone other than Amanda Rabbit.

Then the clouds parted, the sun shone, and two of my repressed, raised-by-wolves brain cells smashed together. This was one of those fabled drag queens, live and in person. I gawked, this time really studying the tall bunny. Her jaw was a little too square, her shoulders too round, and the hair on her chest—WAIT. She had *hair on her chest*, just above the two presidents of her Mount Rushmore.

No one else seemed bothered, but this was one oddity too many for my already whiskey-addled brain. I turned and fled the field as fast as I could. Before I knew it, I was sinking into the safety of Betty's driver's seat and listening to the blessed sound of my door lock clicking into place. My head fell back against the seat rest, and my breathing deepened and slowed.

As I drove home, a slideshow of images scrolled through my head. I couldn't turn it off. A man in fringe dancing with another man in more fringe. Shirtless boys with abs on their toes grinding against each other. A giant bunny looking at me like I was a carrot … never mind. Bad analogy.

What was really odd were the thoughts that followed.

I was terrified of that place. The idea of spending the whole night there without the safety of anyone I knew nearly sent me into a panic attack—and yet, as I thought about it, I hadn't had that much adrenaline-induced fun in a long time. The music was great, and I loved the idea of going from one area to another when my tolerance for country was exceeded.

Oh, and there were men *everywhere*. They came in every age, shape, size, color, and flavor (yes, flavors are a thing, apparently). Many of the men were shirtless and sweaty and rubbing their hands over chests and arms and—

Sorry. Did it just get warm? Why was I sweating? Thinking about all of them made my skin tingle in a way I'd only remembered once before.

Well, twice.

I'd seen Joseph twice.

4

I woke the next day in a pool of sweat. My dreams had been filled with shirtless men grinding against each other, then all turning and looking directly at me while they continued to rub and thrust. Arms reached out, beckoning me to join them on the dance floor. Every guy in the place had that *come-hither* look in their eyes. So I came … I hithered … I henced. I went out there, and a thousand hands tore off my shirt and—

My alarm clock blared.

I rubbed my head and peeled myself off the disgusting sheets and padded into the bathroom. I could smell cigarette smoke on my jeans and shirt from across the room. That was disgusting too. How could fabric absorb that much smoke when I'd never picked up a cigarette in my life?

I showered, tossed last night's smoky laundry into the closet, and threw on some shorts and a T-shirt. The noonday sun was approaching much faster than I'd expected. Some guys from a volleyball game I'd once joined in at the park had talked about sleeping in after a night at the bar. Was this what they meant? I barely felt rested, but the day was almost halfway over.

Midway through my incredibly healthy breakfast of Frosted Flakes, the whirring sound of our old rotary phone broke through my crunching.

I figured it was someone calling for Peter. It usually was. He had a harem, or pack, or posse—I wasn't sure what the right term was for people who hopelessly followed a model around. Men, women, dogs, non-mammals, it didn't matter. He was hot, and they all wanted him; or at least, to be near him so they seemed hotter. I didn't think it really worked that way.

After a couple rings without Peter bounding into the room, I set my spoon down and grabbed the receiver. "Hello?"

"Michael?"

"Yeah. Who's this?"

"It's Dwayne, from the bar—well, from both bars, I guess."

Huh. The old guy was calling the day after he'd abandoned me in a sea of sweaty sensuality.

"Oh hey. Thanks for keeping me company last night. That was … something."

He chuckled. "I bet it was. Are you OK?"

"Yeah, sure, fine." I had no idea why he'd asked that. Why wouldn't I be OK?

He paused a little longer than usual. "You want to grab lunch? I'd love to hear how your evening went. I lost you on the way to the drag show."

I barked a laugh. "Yeah, you did. I tried to find you, but—"

"Sorry. It's impossible to find anyone in that place when it's packed. So, lunch?"

He seemed awfully intent, but I *was* hungry. Tony the Tiger hadn't done my stomach right. "Sure. Why not?"

He suggested we meet at a little diner close to my apartment so we could get breakfast food. Apparently, that's the requisite post-going-out meal. I threw on my holey socks and tennis shoes and headed out.

———

Dwayne was already seated and sipping coffee when I strolled into the diner.

"Hey," I said as I scooted into the seat across from him. It was one of those long booths made for three people on each side. "Planning for the whole bar to join us?"

He grinned. "I took what they gave me. Feel free to stretch out."

The waitress breezed by and gave me the universal *I'll be right back* finger. When I looked back, Dwayne was studying me. I couldn't hold his gaze.

"So, how was last night?" he asked. "Stay long?"

I shrugged and told him about my hiding place by the dance floor. He grinned as I described watching the disco antics. When we got to Miss Bunny, he nearly spat out his coffee.

"You didn't know that was a man dressed up like a woman?" The utter disbelief in his tone matched the upward curl around his eyes. He was loving this.

"I didn't even know there was a theater back there, much

less who was singing." I wanted to be positive, even though the drag had scared the crap out of me. "He—she—I don't really know what to call the singer. They were pretty good. Sounded like the original."

Then he did spit coffee.

He set his mug down and dabbed his shirt in his water glass, then went to work on the spots blooming across his sleeve. His shoulders bobbed with laughter the whole time.

"What's so funny?" I asked.

He looked up and cocked his head, like he was trying to decide something. "You really don't know, do you?" His laughter stilled and he resumed that paternal tone he'd used the night before. "That was a man dressed as a woman, and he was lip-synching, not actually singing. You *were* listening to the original singer."

I opened my mouth to say something, then closed it as the *you're an idiot* feeling crept up my neck.

He smiled. "You really hadn't ever been to a gay bar, had you?"

I shook my head again. "Told you, both were my first bars, gay or otherwise."

"You're what, twenty-two?" he asked.

I stiffened. Not sure why. "I'm twenty-four."

He hid a grin behind a sip of coffee, but I saw it in his eyes.

"Why did you want to have lunch?" I asked, teetering between nervousness and annoyance.

He set his mug down again and leaned back. I could see the wheels turning as he debated how to answer. I don't know what I expected. Maybe he'd flirt. He was gay, right? That's what gay guys did when they were around other dudes—but he was so much older, had to be twenty years older than me. Did old men in their forties still flirt? How did they even still walk around?

"Because you looked like you could use a friend, and I'm a good friend."

Huh. I started to say something witty, but my mouth wouldn't work. His eyes were sincere. There was no leering or lust, just genuine concern and empathy. I might not have understood the whole gay world, but I was good at reading people. Dwayne was being a nice guy.

"Oh. OK. Sure. That's great, I guess." Mouth, please start working.

He chuckled at my fumbling. "Look, you said you're straight, and I'm not looking to win a toaster. I'm being honest. You seem like a decent guy who's a little lost and could use a friend. I like helping younger guys figure things out. That's all."

Figure things out? What did that mean? I was more confused than ever—if that was even possible.

What came out of my mouth next surprised us both. "You don't have a toaster?"

He cocked his head, then the lightbulb turned on and he laughed again. "Sorry, I forget you don't know gay slang. It's a joke. When a gay man converts a straight man, or gets him to have sex, he wins a toaster. Think old days when you got a toaster for opening a bank account."

I felt like I was in a foreign land. "You got a toaster at the bank?"

His mouth opened, but the clatter of waffle-laden plates

slapping the table made us both turn. I'm not sure which of us was more relieved by the waitress's sudden appearance, but it broke the tension. She looked back and forth, obviously sensing something and trying to decipher it. Her brow quirked.

Finally, someone was more confused than me.

The conversation turned to lighter topics. I learned that Dwayne had spent years working as a corporate executive for a company that did something with blood collection or blood banks, I'm wasn't sure, before turning to the simpler life of a waiter in one of Nashville's most exclusive restaurants. I struggled to wrap my head around that transition.

"Why would you leave a cushy corporate job?" I asked.

"I was working ten or twelve-hour days, six days a week. The money was great, but I had no time to spend it. Work *was* life, and that's no way to live." Again, sincerity poured out of his thin frame. I didn't think this guy knew how to be dishonest or insincere.

"But you gave up so much," I said, still puzzling.

He nodded. "It was tough at first, but I've been at the Atrium for years now. They pay well, and the tips are great most nights—but it's the freedom I like more than anything. Yeah, I live in a one-bedroom apartment, but now I can do things I couldn't before—like have lunch with you in the middle of the day."

I nodded like I got it. I didn't.

He asked what I did for work, and I realized I was just as lost and clueless in that part of my life as I'd felt the night before in the bars.

"I work with my dad," I said. "He owns a company that sells private-label products to pharmacies."

It sounded pretty impressive out loud. The truth was far less sexy. We drove more than a thousand miles each week, visiting pharmacies and selling a pain rub my dad had dreamed up from who-knows-where. I love my dad, but he was never the brilliant business guy he thought he was. His little company barely made anything, and my butt and legs ached every night thanks to the endless hours in the car.

"How do you like working with your father?" Dwayne asked.

I shrugged. "It's alright. The best part is I get to spend time with him. I'm the baby in the family, and my parents are older. I probably won't ever get to spend this much time with him again."

I got lost in the implications of that for a moment. Dwayne waited patiently.

"He asked me to work with him while I was still in my senior year at college. It was easier than doing the job search thing and gave me time to figure out what I really wanted to do."

"What *do* you want to do? Wasn't that what college was for? Figuring that out?"

"I guess, but it didn't work. I went in *knowing* I wanted to go to law school. I was really good at debate in college, and the idea of standing in a courtroom with judges and juries was exciting. I dreamed of being the next Perry Mason. Then I met some lawyers and learned they spent more time in the library than the courtroom. I couldn't think of a more painful way to spend my days."

Dwayne cocked his head. "You know who Perry Mason is?"

I laughed. "I'm an old soul, I guess."

"And I'm just old?" He smirked.

I gave him another shrug and the most innocent puppy-dog eyes I could muster.

He laughed harder.

And just like that, Dwayne became my new best friend.

5

———

My dad and I spent the next week roaming all over Alabama.

It's funny. Every small town thinks they're unique and special. I suppose they are in some ways, but I discovered during our gazillion miles on the road that most of them are remarkably similar.

There's a town square—and yes, it usually is either square, with an intersection on each corner, or circular, with roundabout rules that make every driver uneasy. On one side is a law office; on the other, a pharmacy. There are *always* at least two barber shops or beauty salons. The more towns we visited, the more I realized salons and barbershops were more about dissemination of information than styling of hair. Where else could good rumors spread so quickly?

Oh, and don't forget the town's bank, which has been around since before money was invented. The face of the bank is either brick or stone, usually gray, always with the name etched into the face to make it look stable and permanent.

Back then, I was still new to the snake-oil sale, so I'd haul boxes and take notes as my dad marched proudly into each pharmacy and presented his pain rub.

There are salesmen in the world, and then there's my dad. He truly is a category of one.

We would walk into a pharmacy and there would be a pharmacist in a lab coat (always a lab coat). Most of the pharmacists we dealt with were friendly once you got to know them, but had flat personalities. Let's face it, they spent most of their days trying to keep up with the flow of customers and pills without mixing the two up. That would suck the personality out of anyone.

I remember one visit in particular. We walked into a tiny pharmacy barely wide enough for a row of shelves down the middle. The pharmacist was on his knees near the back stocking a shelf. Yes, in a lab coat.

My dad didn't hesitate. He walked up to the pharmacist and introduced himself.

No response. The man kept putting bottles on the shelf.

So my dad launched into his pitch. He told one corny story after another, trying to get the man to laugh or engage—or just turn around.

Nada.

I was starting to wonder why we were still there when my dad turned to me and said, "Put a case on the counter."

I was dumbfounded. The pharmacist had never even acknowledged our presence. But within a minute, an assistant appeared and handed my dad a check.

To this day, I will never know how he did it. If I hadn't believed in magic before, I did in that moment.

That scene repeated itself four or five times each day. That was our life.

FRIDAY FINALLY ROLLED AROUND AND THE TITANIC PULLED back into town. That's what I called my dad's powder-blue Pontiac Bonneville. It was a ship on wheels.

We didn't have cell phones or email back then, so the first thing I always did after a week on the road was check the answering machine. Yes, kids, there was a machine for this. It had a little blinky light that was our version of the endorphin-inducing sound of a text arriving. It rarely blinked for me, but today was my lucky day.

I pressed the button and listened to the whirring of the tape rewinding as I tossed aside my shoes.

"Hey, Michael." It was Dwayne. "Jason's singing down at the Orchid Saturday night. Want to go? I'll protect you from the gays again." I laughed at the same time as he did on the recording, then the click-beep indicating the end of the message sounded. My heart raced as I wondered if Peter was home and had heard Dwayne use the G word. Thankfully, the apartment was empty.

I stripped off my road-wrinkled suit, took a shower, then scavenged for whatever our desert-wasteland-of-a-kitchen might harbor.

Ramen it was.

A few hours and an episode of *MacGyver* later, my mind was divided between utter boredom and the desire to make a nuclear device out of chewing gum and swizzle sticks. I wandered into the bedroom with no clear mission, and found a crumpled wad of paper on the nightstand. Curious, I smoothed it out and held it under my Eiffel Tower bedside lamp. It was Dwayne's name and number. I'd forgotten he'd even given it to me while we were sitting on the patio bar last week. The Connection's name and address was stamped across the top.

For some reason, my heart sped up as I stared at those red letters and numbers.

Images of men line dancing, slow dancing, dancing shirtless, just being shirtless … ugh. Images of men wouldn't get out of my head.

I tossed Dwayne's number aside and tried to walk away, but the magnetic pull of the Connection dragged me back. Before I could think or talk myself out of it, I was pulling on jeans and a ratty white T-shirt. I hadn't really been taking notes last week and missed the memo about the gay-bar uniform. I looked like a poor, straight college student, possibly a homeless one, but I was going to the bar.

STANDING IN LINE AT A GAY BAR WAS A LITTLE INTIMIDATING. Most of the guys were normal- looking dudes just hoping to have fun on a Friday night, but some of them looked like they should've been in front of a camera, not a bar queue. I'd never really noticed how hot a guy was before, but now I couldn't stop looking—and staring. My head was spinning faster than a propellor on a prop plane. The guy behind me had to nudge me with his elbow when it was my turn to pay the doorman.

I wandered into the hallway to find it nearly empty, so I ducked into the entrance I knew led to the country bar and outdoor patio. One guy was practicing his line dancing to some twangy song I didn't recognize. The clomp-clomp of his boots echoed through the nearly empty space. Two older, snow-topped men huddled at the bar, reminding me of the old guys in the balcony from the Muppets.

Hey, don't laugh. Miss Piggy was cool. I had her lunchbox in third grade. *Pigs in Space* rocked.

I turned to the bar to find Cowboy Rick smiling knowingly. I tried to look confident as I ambled up to him, but every eye in the place turned in my direction, even Mr. Clompity's. I was suddenly very uncomfortable.

"Pretty boy, you came back."

My head must've snapped up a little too fast, or my eyes were too wide or something, because the Muppets and Cowboy Rick broke into a fit of laughter.

The fourteen shades of red I turned probably didn't help. Rick at least attempted to stifle his laughter, but the Muppets were unrestrained. I wanted to slink away, but there was nowhere to hide.

Rick leaned over, doing the *look at my muscular arms flex* thing I'd seen last week. His biceps were like softballs tearing at the fabric of his fringe-covered shirt. Damn.

"Eyes up here," he said, with too much mirth in his voice. Then he lowered his volume to a whisper only I could hear. "Honey, you're new, aren't you?"

Somehow my eyes widened further as I nodded nervously.

He put a hand on my arm. I shivered.

"It's alright. We were all new once, even those old goats." He motioned with a nod to the Muppets. "If you get nervous or uncomfortable, you come back to my bar. I'll make sure none of the big bad bears get you, OK?"

He had that same kind paternal look I'd seen on Dwayne's face, despite being only a year or two older than me. He wasn't flirting. He was being nice.

I let out a breath. "Thanks. Is it that obvious?"

He chuckled. "Well, you didn't pee the dance floor, so I'd say you're doing just fine. Doesn't hurt you look like *that*." He eyed me up and down.

I looked down at my shirt, specifically the holes in it. "Uh, it was clean." I gave him a sheepish look.

He laughed again. "I wasn't talking about your shirt, silly. Nobody cares about that here. Half the shirts come off at midnight anyway. I was just saying you're handsome, and that helps in a place like this."

The fifteenth shade of red found its way to my face. He thought *I* was handsome? I couldn't believe it. I was always that skinny kid, the one with the pasty skin who couldn't tan. I'd never thought of myself as handsome. I still couldn't see myself that way.

But a gay bartender with bulging biceps in tan fringe said I was, so it *must* be true, right?

Rick suddenly turned away and started making a drink. I looked around, but there wasn't anyone new. When I turned back, two shot glasses stared up at me with some kind of pinkish liquid inside.

"Sex on the Beach. Do it with me?"

I nearly fell off the stool. "What? You want … what?"

Rick nearly peed the dance floor. One of the Muppets knocked his drink over as he gasped for breath between snorts.

"It's the name of the drink," Rick said through tears. "I was asking if you'd drink one with me."

"Oh." I looked down at the drink, desperate to avoid eye contact with anyone within earshot. "Uh, sure, I guess."

"You're new to drinking too, aren't you?" Rick asked as I

took a ladylike sip. "Down the hatch." He threw his head back and his drink vanished.

I followed his lead.

"I can't let your first shot be a misfire. One more?" He didn't wait for an answer.

The second shot didn't burn like the first one had. I don't remember feeling it at all.

As Rick reached for my empty glass, I asked, "Where is everybody? It was packed last week."

"Give it an hour. You're early."

I looked up at the neon Busch beer clock behind the bar. It read ten-thirty.

One of the Muppets surprised me by gripping my forearm. "Honey, nobody but us old farts comes here before eleven. You'll figure it all out." He patted my arm and the pair headed out, leaving me alone with Rick and Mr. Clompity.

RICK KEPT ME COMPANY UNTIL THE TRICKLE OF NEW ARRIVALS turned into a steady stream. A little before midnight, the stream became an uncontrollable flood of man-flesh. I stepped away from the bar and took a seat just outside on the patio, where I could watch. I'd never seen so many people hug each other. Was that a gay thing? Were they all related somehow, or did they just like hugging?

The Busch clock actually poured a golden shower of neon when midnight struck. Pretty cool. I took the cue from the gay-bar gods and wandered into the main dance floor area. It was just as packed as the week before. I threaded my way through the crowd to my secret corner and felt the security of the wall behind me as I leaned back.

Time to watch the animals at the zoo.

The lights were pretty much off, with swirling strobes and spotlights that gave the warehouse a feeling of dizzying motion. It was a little hard to focus on faces with all the lights flashing, but after a few eye blinks, things cleared up. The thrum of the bass reverberated in my chest. It danced with the anxious nerves bouncing around in there, keeping them company and out of my head. I'd never get used to the over-powering stench of cigarettes, but my nose did stop twitching after about ten minutes. My clothes were really going to stink again.

I got bored watching the same guys dance and decided to wander. The show bar was still fairly empty. A few older men huddled around the bar, a pattern I was beginning to under-stand. There were a handful of small groups congregated around tables, laughing, chatting and drinking. Everyone looked so happy.

I stared up at the nearly empty balcony and curiosity drove my feet up the stairs. A bored bartender slumped against the glossy surface of his counter. Two guys huddled at a table in the corner, kissing between childlike giggles. If I looked young, they looked twelve.

Noises from below called to me, so I peered over the railing to find the best view in the house. I could see the stage and catwalk, and even the bar below, although some of the guys were merely tops of heads from this vantage point. Guys wandered in and out of the room, seemingly as curious or bored as I had been, but few remained still for long. Looking down gave the place a feeling of energy. It crawled with it—or maybe the people were doing the crawling, I wasn't sure.

I'd lost myself in a voyeuristic trance when an arm bumped against mine, and a voice with more treble than bass spoke. "Hey."

I turned to find an absolutely beautiful blond bombshell of a man standing next to me. My eyes involuntarily dropped to the fishnet-looking shirt he was wearing. I think there was actually more skin than net. While I didn't exactly share his fashion sense, the bulging chest and rippling abs made my already tight jeans pinch a bit more. It must've been cold because his nipples were poking through the net and staring at me.

"Hey," I said artfully. My eyes took their time rising to meet his.

He smiled. Damn. He had *perfect* teeth that practically glowed in the black light of the bar, but I couldn't see what color his eyes were. "You look bored. Want to get out of here?"

I nearly jumped off the balcony. "Uh, what? Leave? Now? I mean … I just got here." I gulped in air. "But, just curious, where were you thinking of going?"

He didn't hesitate. "My condo. It's way more fun than this place."

It wasn't even midnight and this guy wanted to leave. I mean, he was crazy-hot, but did guys just meet up like this and leave together? At least Joseph and I saw a movie first, got to know each other. I was a little baffled, but couldn't stop looking at the abs he'd caught in his net. For once, the little angel on my shoulder had laryngitis, while the devil was dancing an Irish jig.

"OK. I'm kinda bad with directions though. Can I just follow you?"

His teeth flashed again. "Sure."

He grabbed my hand and pulled me along like a little red wagon until we entered the parking lot. I'd never held a guy's hand before, certainly not in public, but no one seemed to notice—except for Cowboy Rick, who was taking a ciggie break by the door as we walked out. He gave me the strangest chuckle and shook his head, then waved with four fingers like he was tickling the air.

The cool, nicotine-free air outside filled my lungs. It was a full moon—naturally—and I now had my first well-lit view of the guy dragging me to my doom.

Holy Mother of Hotness and Sin, Batman.

He was flawless. Whoever chiseled his jaw needed a prize or trophy or whatever they gave chiselers of stuff. In the light, there was even less fishnet and more flesh, if that was possible —and how were his jeans tighter than mine? How was *that* possible? He could crack walnuts with his butt cheeks; they were poking out in their perfect rounded glory through his denim. One back pocket was ripped and flapping, and there was no fabric covering his pale, hairless skin. God bless his wardrobe malfunction.

He walked me to where Betty waited, gave me the appropriate reaction for one who'd never seen a Saturn, then vanished across the sea of cars to retrieve his own. A moment later, he pulled up in a sporty green BMW convertible, top down, golden hair flowing, teeth flashing. My heart raced as he pulled up beside me.

He didn't speak, just grinned and motioned with his hand for me to follow.

6

Halfway to Blondie's house, the little angel decided to wake up and start peeping in my ear. What a nag. For a split second, my preacher's kid guilt kicked in, and I thought about turning Betty around and heading home. Then the little devil licked my lobe and the hard-on that had started as we left Connection threatened to rip my zipper open. I thumped that angel so hard she slammed against the back windshield. I was sure I'd pay for that at some point in life, but not that night.

We pulled up to a blocky brick warehouse with faded lettering across the top that read Nashville Steel. I didn't even know we made steel. Does one even *make* steel? Or shape it? Or melt it? I have no idea. I had even less idea why we were parking at a steel factory. Plant. Warehouse. Steel place.

Anyway.

Blondie flicked his hair back and grinned lecherously, then gave me the *come-hither* finger. Like a dumbass, I nodded and waved from across the parking lot like some kid who'd just spotted his mom picking him up from school. He chuckled.

We walked inside and I couldn't stop gawking at the

girders and beams that rose and crisscrossed everywhere. The place was seriously cool. Blondie noticed and explained. "This used to be a factory where they made steel parts for ships and river boats, but was abandoned years ago when the company went under. Some developer bought it and turned it into open-concept condos. I think I was actually the first person to get one."

He seemed very proud of being the first. I resisted the urge to ask what an open-concept condo was.

We were halfway down the eternal hallway when he stopped at the third door. As we entered, I was again in gawker heaven. The same girders latticed the ceiling, making the place feel old, incredibly tall, and somehow new at the same time. There were no walls, just one massive room with a few of those folding divider-screen things I remembered seeing in Asian movies. On one side was a modern-looking kitchen with shiny silver appliances and countertops that looked like medical examination tables. The middle held a long L-shaped leather sectional and flat screen that covered most of the wall. Outside of a movie theater, I had never seen a screen that wide. It was powered on when we entered. The screen saver flipped between landscapes and ocean views—a really nice touch.

Against the wall opposite the kitchen was a sprawling king-sized bed with a mattress that barely rose to my waist. An antique-looking wrought-iron frame swooped in artistic waves above layers of pillows. The contrast between the frame and the brick of the wall was very cool.

I couldn't get over how open the open concept really was. Even the toilet and shower were exposed. The shower head poked out of a concrete slab that reminded me of some bad high school football TV show where half the scenes were of guys showering after practice. I was fascinated and started walking over to see how he kept water from flooding every-where without a shower curtain.

Before I made it three steps, strong hands gripped my arms, spun me around, and shoved me against a steel beam. Warm lips attacked mine, and a tongue darted between my now open mouth. Blondie was all passion and fire, an urgency driving him to action, and I knew there wouldn't be any small talk—probably no talk at all.

I thought my heart was going to beat out of my chest.

While his tongue explored, his fingers found the end of my T-shirt. Before I could think, white fabric ripped over my head and flew across the room, smacking against the oh-so-dry shower. I fumbled with his shirt, desperate to feel his skin against mine, but the fishnet was awkward and my fingers got stuck. He looked down, then back up at the embarrassment in my eyes, and barked a laugh.

I thought the mood might've been broken, but his laugh fell away, and he pressed his lips into my neck. A shiver ran from my neck to my toes, and I let out a soft moan. I felt him grind against me.

He unwound the stringy netting from my digits and loos-ened his shirt, dropping it unceremoniously where we stood.

Sweet baby Jesus.

He was even more perfect than I'd thought. His abs were harder than the beam pressing into my back. I couldn't remember ever seeing anyone with such a perfect physique. I reached up and pressed my hand to his chest. It didn't budge. It was like pressing that concrete shower wall, but with tiny pink nipples that begged to be nibbled. I ran my fingers across his arms and could feel the separation of each muscle. He wasn't ogreish like some bodybuilders; he was lean and thick and hard.

In a flash, so was I. Hard, that is.

He reached up and closed my mouth, his eyes glittering, then hooked one finger into the top of my jeans above the button and pulled. Like a pup on a leash, I let him tug me toward the bed. I could barely think. Was this really happening?

When we reached the edge of the bed, he dropped to his knees and took the button of my jeans in his mouth. His face brushed against my stomach and I couldn't stop a shiver. Through some otherworldly gay sorcery, he unbuttoned and unzipped my Wranglers with his teeth. I rarely wore underwear, and his tongue found more than he likely expected as the denim parted. Wide eyes looked up, smiling once again.

I reached down to help remove my jeans, but he gripped my hands, his hold firm. "Tonight, you *only* do what I tell you, alright?"

I wasn't sure what that meant, so I nodded and didn't say anything. He released my hands and gripped my jeans, pulling them down as slowly as he could. He turned his head and rubbed his cheek against where my erection was sprouting.

I can still remember the smooth softness of his skin against mine. I wanted him so badly in that moment.

When my jeans finally found my ankles, his mouth had consumed every inch of me. His head rose and fell as he ran lips and tongue up and down my shaft. I spasmed every time the tip pressed against the back of his throat. He pressed further, willing me deeper inside him. I ran my fingers through his hair while he licked and sucked. He reached up and gripped my chest, then trailed his fingers firmly down my stomach and abs.

Finally, he leaned back and pushed me onto the bed. I flopped onto my back and tried to lean forward, but he pushed me back. "No moving unless I tell you to, remember?"

I nodded frantically.

He finished removing my jeans, then straightened my body so I was laying with my head on a pillow. He was still wearing his jeans, but I could see his excitement throbbing down one leg. He hung to the right. I wanted to reach up and feel it, but he'd told me not to move, and I was a good boy.

"Stay there. I'll be right back," he said with a quick kiss to my nipple.

A moment later, he was back with one hand held secretively behind him. "Close your eyes."

I did as he commanded.

There was a pause and the sound of shuffling. I felt warmth above me as his naked flesh hovered. He crawled up the bed, and his dick dangled and brushed against my own. I could feel the skin of his uncut cock as it pulled back slightly with my touch. Something wet moistened my head.

Then silky cloth covered my eyes, and I flinched.

"Shh. Don't move."

His mouth was over mine, breathing into me, as he tied the silk behind my head. He kissed me deeply, then the heat of his body vanished as I felt his weight leave the mattress.

"Put your arms out like you're reaching for the corners of the bed."

What the f—?

My breath caught, then quickened. Sweat bloomed across my chest and forehead, and my heart thumped faster.

I did as he commanded.

Before I could ask what he was doing, both wrists felt the same tight pull of silk my face had a moment earlier. I tried to lower them, but found they'd been tied to the iron headboard and wouldn't budge. Fear jolted down my spine. What had I done coming here with this guy? How could I have been so stupid? I started to panic and tried pulling against the silk, but was shocked into stillness by the sensation of warm liquid dribbling across my chest and stomach.

"Relax. *Trust me.* I won't hurt you."

I *wanted* to believe him. He was so freakin' hot, and I had twenty-four years of pent-up repression begging for wild, crazy sex—but this man had me blindfolded and tied to a bed. My rational mind was screaming to grab my clothes and run as fast as I could.

Then he pressed his slick body against mine and all rational thought vanished.

He'd apparently rubbed himself down with the same oil he'd dripped on me, and our bodies slid with frictionless ease. His hands ran up my sides, spreading oil everywhere, tickling and teasing as his tongue and teeth reached my neck. I could feel his erection pressing just under my balls, and my back arched.

My whole body trembled. The fear of being bound and blinded by a stranger somehow heightened my other senses, and ripples of pleasure bloomed everywhere his skin touched. He kissed me. No, he *devoured* me, his tongue exploring mine again and again. When our dicks slid against each other, I thought I might explode. My body shook and my breathing heaved.

He pulled back, and the heat of his touch cooled. I could hear him at the foot of the bed.

The mattress dipped as I felt him crawl across the bed on his knees. Oily fingertips traced across my skin, starting at my ankle, up my calf to the inside of my thigh. Then he did it again up both legs at the same time. It tickled and tingled. I could picture his chest and arms, see his fingers touching me, feel his lips, though they were far away.

I clenched, caught off guard, when his finger teased my butt, barely grazing the tiny hairs outside my hole, then pressed inside. I heard a *pop* as his finger came out, then a chuckle. When his finger didn't return for more exploration, I began to wonder if I'd done something wrong. I lifted my head to listen for him. Then I felt the heat of his breath, and my hole quivered. His tongue was hot and wet, and the oil let it slide in without protest. He pressed into me, testing, then thrusted it harder and deeper.

I moaned again, louder. I sucked in a breath as my world spun.

"God, you're tight," he said, as he pulled his tongue out, teased around the edges, then plunged it even deeper and more insistent. His hands went from gentle to gripping, squeezing and releasing my hips, pulsing in time with the rhythm his tongue.

I groaned when he finally pulled back. How could he ever stop that? I wanted him to keep licking and pressing and squeezing. I couldn't imagine anything feeling better than his tongue—

Until, without warning, he slid inside me.

No one had ever been inside me.

With all the oil and sweat, he slipped inside me like he'd

been there all his life. I cried out and he stopped, a hand pressed against my chest.

"Don't stop."

"Ask me nicely." His voice carried amusement and desire, an alluring cocktail.

"Please, get back inside me and don't ever pull out. I need you inside me," I pleaded.

"That's my boy."

He eased back slowly, then slammed into me again, this time deeper, driving the breath out of me. I gripped the silk holding my hands, and fear mingled with pleasure as I remembered being tied—but I didn't care anymore. I'd given myself to him, to his pleasure, and he could have whatever he wanted.

My back arched. My toes clenched. He retreated then plunged into me as he pulled my cheeks apart with his hands. The hardness of his pelvis pressed urgently against my hips. He wanted to be as deep as possible in me, and I wanted it too. He *couldn't* get deep enough.

His tip pressed against some fleshy barrier. It resisted him, held him back. He pressed deeper. I felt him lean over and grip my shoulders for leverage, then press again. Something relaxed inside me, and he entered a place I never knew existed. I groaned, and waves of ecstasy rolled where shivers had trailed moments before.

A deep growl rumbled with his groan, driving my senses further into madness. He held himself deep inside me, unmoving, and his hands rubbed my legs, then pressed against my chest. I could feel him hardening even more inside me.

That excited me.

His lips brushed against mine, and I reached up to kiss him. He pulled back to keep us a breath apart, then I felt the silk pull away from my eyes and I could see his face inches from mine.

God, he was beautiful and fierce and *intense*. His eyes were infinite pools of blue brimming with passion and fire, hunger and need. His gaze bore into my soul. No one had ever looked into me like that.

My heart leapt into my throat.

He saw the shift and pressed his lips hard against my mouth, then began grinding himself into me. Wrapping his arms around me, his body melded with my own. The oil heated with our skin, and his thrusting sped up. He raised himself to his knees and held my legs in the air. His chest was slick, and light flickered off his abs.

His eyes never left mine.

He quickened. His thrusts were deep and desperate. I moaned and threw my head back as I felt his body tensing. He was close. I wanted him, all of him. He didn't slow. His hand gripped me and began stroking, his fingers squeezing and caressing from base to tip. He was gentle and firm, the oil giving him permission. He was inside me, raging. He pressed deeper and faster, until finally his head flew back and he released a primal cry. I felt the thrill as he flowed into me. His whole body pulsed as wave after wave left him.

He kept himself inside me and wrapped his hand around my shaft once more. This time, it didn't take long. My body tensed and I felt myself explode across his abs. Through overwhelmed senses, I heard him cry out again, and felt him release a second time, somehow in perfect unison with my own cry.

He smiled, ran a hand across my chest again, then laid his body on top of mine.

7

____

"We fell asleep like that, me tied up, his body spread across mine. I could still feel him pulsing inside me as I fell asleep."

Dwayne and I sat in the corner of the diner. It was a rustic eatery whose tables were level-ish, thanks to stacks of sugar packets shoved under their legs. It didn't look like much, but the food was good and cheap.

"So, what was the guy's name? When are you going to see him again? Tell me more." Dwayne leaned forward on his elbows.

Shit.

He saw the panicked look on my face and started laughing. "You don't remember his name, do you?"

"It's worse than that."

"Oh Lord. What?"

"I never got his name. All I know is—well, I'm *assuming* —he's a flight attendant. There were a bunch of uniform coats with wings in his closet."

Dwayne struggled to come up for air as his laughter drew

looks from other tables. "You let a hot flight attendant whose name you never got fuck your brains out and cum inside you?" He doubled over.

I couldn't help but laugh with him. Before I knew it, we were both giggling through tears as the waitress appeared.

"Care to share?" she asked with a smile.

Dwayne started to say something, but I cut him off with a horrified stare. "No! Sorry, it's an inside joke."

"*Inside* joke. That's priceless!" Dwayne nearly choked on the laughter following that faux pas.

The waitress refilled our tea and scurried away. I think we scared the poor girl.

"So, did you and Fly Boy talk at all?" Dwayne asked through gasps.

"Does grunting and moaning count?"

He couldn't get his tea glass to his mouth fast enough and had to set it down before it spilled. "You didn't even talk at all? Seriously?"

"Well, I tried. When we got to his place, I started to ask about the building, but he threw me against the wall and any thought of steel or smelting went out the window."

"Oh, I'm pretty sure your mind was on steel." He was riding this harder than Fly Boy had. "What about in the morning, before you left?"

I shook my head. "I woke up in the middle of the night, got dressed, and left. He was out of it, so we didn't talk then either."

"Did you at least get to keep one of his ties as a souvenir?"

I couldn't help but chuckle. "No. All I got was to be his baby mama."

He scowled.

Now I was confused. That had been a pretty witty comeback.

"Michael, we need to talk about that." He crossed his arms and leaned back.

Uh-oh. No good conversation ever begins with *we need to talk*. Anyone who's ever watched a movie knows the greatest breakups in history have followed that phrase. This little brunch was about to take a serious turn.

I shifted uncomfortably in the squeaky booth.

"You let him cum inside you. You know you can't let guys do that. *Ever*."

Here I'd just told Dwayne about a rock-my-world experience with a guy, basically admitting I was gay, and he was *scolding* me? I barely knew how to react. Plus, I didn't really understand what I'd done wrong. Sure, it was random sex with a guy whose name I never asked—and he never offered. The whole night went against pretty much everything I was raised to believe, but damn, it was hot. I thought the Gay Handbook encouraged random hook-ups, like it was part of the culture, or a man's rite of passage.

Gay rules were confusing.

His face morphed from concerned to annoyed when I didn't immediately turn contrite. "HIV, Michael."

"Huh? What about HIV?"

He cocked his head as if examining a baby bird. "You don't know *anything*, do you?"

I gave him my best puppy-dog eyes, the ones that usually got me out of trouble with him. They didn't work.

I really *didn't* know anything.

"Unprotected sex is one of the chief ways HIV spreads. I used to work in a blood bank. I know all about this stuff. Hell,

I watched too many friends get sick and die. The press doesn't talk about AIDS like they used to, but it's still raging out there, taking great people before their time. Even if it doesn't kill you, you'd have to take meds for the rest of your life, and who knows how other guys would react to you? People are still ignorant and scared. I don't want to watch any of that happen to you."

I lowered my gaze. "Sorry. I didn't know."

"You don't owe *me* an apology, silly, but you *need* to know these things before you go out into the big gay world and stick your butt in the air like a horny hyena."

I couldn't help the mental image that popped into my head. Tea flew out my mouth. "A horny hyena?"

He smirked and shrugged. "I'm just worried about you. This whole life is new to you, and I don't want to see you pay for an innocent mistake. It could cost you your life."

I looked up and saw the most heartfelt concern in his eyes. He wasn't exactly a father figure, despite being old enough to actually *be* my father. I thought of Dwayne more like an older brother. There was zero attraction on my part, but I felt compelled to be around him, to be close and share with him. It's hard to explain. From the day we met, he'd felt special, like family.

He reached across the table and put his hand on my arm. "I don't mean to lecture, and I know we've only known each other a few weeks, but you're important to me."

"Thanks. Really." I put my hand on his and gulped back the emotion threatening to emerge. "I never would've dealt with any of these feelings if you hadn't shown up at that bar to see Jason. You've been so patient and listened, even when I talked out my ass about being straight."

Shit. Did I just say that?

He studied me a moment, then said in his most serious tone, "You're still straight, right?"

I laughed, suddenly nervous. Did he want me to say it out loud, to admit I really did like boys, like Jason had asked that first night? I wasn't sure I could get the word out. I wasn't ready to be that honest with him—*or myself.*

I just rolled with it. "Yep, still straight as an arrow."

"That's what I thought." He raised his glass in salute.

8

———

I drove back to my apartment, climbed the steps, and stared at the door. Peter was probably inside.

My gut churned. I was excited from the night before. Talking about it over lunch was almost the same as getting to live it all over again. Well, not really, but it was fun seeing the shock on Dwayne's face as I told him about the silk ties. *I* was still in shock from the first kiss of them on my wrists.

As giddy as I might've been from getting laid—I mean, *seriously* laid—there was a part of me that felt a stab of guilt. I couldn't help it. The preacher's kid would always live inside me, and sometimes he decided to stand up and shout. I wished he would just stay quiet and let me have fun. I'd never had fun like this before. Guilt made it, I don't know … less.

Then I felt silly standing outside my own apartment. Peter wouldn't know anything, other than I hadn't come home until after lunch the next day, if he was even awake himself. Why was I so worried what he thought anyway? Sure, I had a bit of a crush on him. Everyone did. Women, men, even straight guys crushed on him. He was *that* hot and that likable.

So why did my gut clench thinking about facing him?

Would he ask where I'd been? I couldn't tell him I'd gone to a gay bar and hooked up with some random dude, could I? He didn't know I was gay. Hell, I couldn't even admit it myself when Dwayne had asked me earlier. Why did everything have to be so confusing?

I ran my hands through my hair and shouldered through the door.

"Hey. Where've you been?" Peter looked up from his perch at the kitchen bar. He was stuffing half a pound cake in his mouth. I know, weird. He was convinced he could eat as much pound cake as he wanted—as a meal substitute—and his abs would never disappear. And yes, *he* was coaching others on being healthy. That's my Peter.

"Had brunch with a friend. You?"

He snorted through bites. "I meant last night. You never came home."

I tried not to fidget, but I was sure my ears were turning red. "Oh, well, I went out, you know, to a bar."

He set the cake down. Crap. His eyes had acquired missile lock, and I could tell by his smirk he was about to fire. "Huh."

That's it? That was all he was going to say? I scooted past him, desperate to reach my room before he could get off a good shot.

I heard a loud sniffing sound, then he spoke again. "Cigarette smoke mixed with … something. Perfume? Cologne? I recognize that one."

Of course he did. He was the gayest straight guy ever to sashay up to the men's fragrance counter.

I ignored him and tried to stay casual as I darted into my room and slammed the door.

OK, that wasn't exactly casual. I panicked.

Once inside the safety of my personal space, I smelled something awful and realized I needed a shower. My jeans were stuck to my leg from Fly Boy's, um, *cologne*.

Crap.

Crap. Crap. Crap.

Neither of our rooms connected to the bathroom. It was down the short hall, but would force me to pass near him as he sat on his throne of judgment in the kitchen.

I almost made it.

"What was her name?" an amused sounding, cake-muffled voice asked.

I froze. He thought I'd hooked up with *a girl*. Perfect.

"Uh, well, she was really hot."

Nice. *Smooth*. Idiot.

He laughed and I could see bits of cake fly across the bar. "You don't know her name? Seriously? My preacher's kid?" His laughter grew into a full-blown giggle fit.

I hated him.

Not really. I secretly wanted to get in his pants.

Wait, did he just use the possessive *my* when referring to me? My heart fluttered. "Hey, I'm a rock star. What can I say?"

He guffawed as I disappeared into the safety of the bathroom and locked the door. We never locked doors, but I needed it bolted, chained and sealed in that moment. I leaned back and closed my eyes, trying to remember to breathe. I'd *never* lied to Peter before. Now I felt guilty about that too. Perfect.

A few minutes later, as I was finally peeling off my vile

jeans, Peter's voice boomed through the door, nearly startling me into the tub.

"I'm headed to work. In all the excitement of your midnight romp, I forgot to tell you some guy called right before you got home. Dwayne? Number's on the pad by the phone."

"OK, thanks," I yelled back.

Peter's footsteps faded, then the door slammed as he exited our apartment. I could finally soak in a comforting waterfall. The water was hotter than usual. Maybe I was trying to scorch the guilt off my body, along with Fly Boy's children. I don't know. I didn't feel the heat, but my skin was angry when I toweled off and glanced in the mirror. I dropped the towel and studied myself, something I never did.

Like I told you before, I'd always been the scrawny toothpick who couldn't tan. Really attractive, right? Self-conscious didn't come close to describing how I felt about myself, especially about my body—but standing there, sans towel, after a night of silk-bound sex that had been hotter than my shower water, I gazed at myself and, for the first time in my life, thought *I* looked kind of hot. Peter's incessant whip-crack at the gym had helped round my shoulders and chest, and my arms were no longer rail-thin reeds. My stomach had always been flat, but I'd never eaten well enough to reveal abs—and I'd certainly never inflicted crunch-style pain on myself to form them—but there they were, poking through, smiling up at me.

I flexed, impressed, then laughed at my ridiculous Arnold pose. I actually looked pretty good naked. I'd *never* thought that about myself before.

A strange warmth bloomed in my chest, and my hand

reflexively rose to touch it. I traced my fingers across the compact muscle that hadn't existed a few months earlier. I squeezed my bicep as my hand moved across it and grinned at the firm ball that formed.

Then the rusty tint in my hair caught my eye in the mirror and the moment burst like an overinflated balloon. I might only be half-ginger, but that's enough to be skittish as hell. What can I say? All gingers see their hair as hottie kryptonite, sealing us away from ever being among the truly beautiful.

Genetics aside, I'll never forget that moment, that glimpse of who I was becoming, what my body was becoming. Pride I'd never known—that I'd never known could even exist—about myself sparked to life.

It took a while to wipe the goofy grin from my face.

FRESHLY SHOWERED AND CHANGED, I WANDERED INTO THE DEN and flipped on the TV. Bowling. *Star Trek*. A documentary about coral reefs. Awesome.

I remembered Peter's shout about Dwayne calling and decided whatever he had to talk about was better than tenpin, so I grabbed the phone and spun the numbers. Yes, kids, it was an old-school rotary phone. If you don't know what I'm talking about, I'm embarrassed for you.

"Hello?"

"Hey, Dwayne. It's Michael."

"Oh hey. Thanks for brunch today. I realized after we left that you paid the bill. You didn't have to do that."

I really couldn't afford it either, but he'd paid for the last couple. My guilt was now a hat trick. "No problem. Happy to."

There was an awkward pause.

"So, Jason is playing another gig tonight at the Orchid. Please don't make me sit through another three hours of the same songs by myself." He and Jason had been friends for years, and I knew he'd go to any performance our illustrious singer invited him to attend, but he sounded a little desperate for company.

"Sure. I don't have anything going on tonight, and you know how dangerous it is to leave me alone on a Saturday."

He chuckled. That was an inside joke between us now. "That's an understatement," he said. "Meet you there at seven?"

"Sure. I'll eat before we get there though. Peter's got me watching my food, and I'm finally noticing a difference. Don't want to blow it."

I had to pull the receiver away from my ear as his laughter barked through. "Oh, I'm starting to think you want to *blow* everything."

My ears turned red again, I was sure of it. "Ha ha. Very funny. Although, if they all look like Fly Boy …"

"Oh stop! They don't count if you don't get their name. New rule."

"He didn't *need* to count. He just needed to use his tongue—"

"Enough! I'm done with you. See you tonight." Click.

I chuckled. I might not have admitted I was gay yet, but I didn't seem to have any trouble talking about having a man's tongue shoved up my ass, and getting mild-mannered Dwayne to hang up on me had been quite the accomplishment.

<hr>

SEVEN O'CLOCK ROLLED AROUND QUICKLY. DWAYNE MET ME on the sidewalk outside the Wild Orchid, a local bar that packed in the crowds for their live music. The place was famous for discovering any number of successful singers, and everyone working their way up the chain in Nashville wanted to perform on that stage. Dwayne told me it was fairly common for producers and talent scouts to show up unannounced on weekends. Whether they liked the food or were actually looking for singers was unclear. I was a little surprised Jason had landed such a prime gig on a Saturday night, but I really didn't know much about the music scene other than what Dwayne had explained in our time together.

We'd only made it a couple steps inside when Hurricane Jason blew up to us and wrapped Dwayne in an embrace. "Dwayne! Thanks for coming. You're my *only* fan here tonight."

Dwayne looked sideways at me, and Jason followed his eyes.

"Oh hey." He had that look on his face like he recognized me from somewhere, but couldn't remember where. "Were you—"

I saved him. "We work out at the same gym, and Dwayne invited me to hear you sing a couple weeks ago. You're really good."

He beamed at the compliment and the memory-scowl vanished. "Why, thank you." It sounded like his practiced reply to a compliment regarding a performance. He was always on stage, I guessed.

"Gotta go get ready for my set. The table up front with the

reserved card is for you." He hugged Dwayne one more time, then snaked his way through the tables to the side door by the stage. Dwane shrugged, and I followed him to our promised table. Jason wasn't kidding; we were in the front row, practically bumping against the stage.

Dwayne leaned over. "I hate it when he sticks me under his nose. Let's get a different table. I'll tell him the house needed the prime spot for someone important."

He motioned a waitress and a moment later we were comfortable, midway back and against a wall. Dwayne had been right. We had been pretty much up the performer's nose.

Dwayne ordered a pork chop that made my stomach growl. I got an iced tea and munched on the bowl of bar snacks we'd sweet-talked out of the waitress. Being friends with the artist had its advantages, sometimes in tasty, garlicky nuts.

Stop snickering and get your mind out of the gutter. I'd never tasted Jason's nuts.

We chatted and laughed. Dwayne told me about some new boy who'd started waiting tables at his fancy restaurant. Jeff was twenty-two, had wavy blond hair and emerald eyes. Dwayne got a faraway look when he described how he'd sauntered into the restaurant in his 'Ducks in a Row' T-shirt from the Peabody Hotel in Memphis. Apparently, the shirt was cute and a little too tight, two things Dwayne loved in a man half his age.

In the short time we'd known each other, he'd only mentioned two guys, and both were under the age of twenty-five. Dwayne was forty-one.

I listened patiently, then launched a barrage of playful attacks at my friend's need for an ankle bracelet near schools.

He snorted unapologetically and waved me off. "I can't help it if I like younger guys," he countered.

"Grass on the field, play ball?"

He gave me a sharp look.

"Old enough to pee, old enough for me?"

This earned me a smack on the arm as the waitress appeared.

"Help! This old coot's attacking me. Call Child Protective Services, quick!"

She glanced between us with raised brows as she refilled my tea. Dwayne smacked me again. "Somebody has to keep these youngsters in line," he quipped without missing a beat.

We both laughed, and the poor waitress shook her head, a tiny curl threatening the corner of her mouth. She was in for a long night. At least we'd be entertaining.

Someone tapped the microphone, saving Dwayne from more teasing and my arm from his punches. We turned to watch and listen.

There was a mic stand, a bar stool, and Jason on a raised, round stage barely wide enough for two performers. He stepped up to the microphone with a wide leather guitar strap crossing his shoulder, the instrument cradled in his hands. He strummed a few chords, smiled, then looked out toward the crowd. Light applause returned his greeting as diners divided their attention between the stage and their meals.

I'd seen Jason several times at the gym, usually in a tank top and skimpy shorts. From what I saw, he was in great shape, and was a generally handsome guy—but it was his smile and the magnetic way he drew people toward him that I noticed more than anything. He had this mystical pull. People *wanted* to be near him, to interact with him, to be seen by him. I'd been fascinated by the phenomena a few times while doing leg presses or arm curls. I hadn't been smitten so much as fascinated. I figured that was a required gift for a performer, at least one with any shot at making it in the business.

Charisma is a funny thing.

As Jason started singing, I looked at him. No, not like any old fan in the audience. I *really* looked at him. In some ways, it felt like the first time. His voice smiled with each note, the lyrics recalling happy memories in Austin around Lake Travis, giving the audience a virtual hug filled with warmth. His face, to those who knew him, carried a hint of longing and pain. I leaned forward. Yes, that *was* pain, or, more accurately, heartache. Someone he'd cared for and spent time with on Lake Travis wasn't in his life anymore.

How did I know this? Was I channeling Celine Dion? Or the other Celine? Or Dionne? I get them confused.

I *felt* every word, every note. His pain drifted into my heart and pulled at my soul. I wanted to leap out of my chair, knock Dwayne's pork chop to the floor, and race into Jason's waiting arms to comfort him. He needed me, I knew it.

Damn you, Lake Travis! How dare you hurt my Jason!

The screechy sound of a vinyl record being scratched sounded in my head. You know, that cringe-worthy sound that literally stops life? *My Jason?* Where the hell had that come from?

I looked back up to the stage as he finished his song and gave a shallow bow to the crowd's polite applause. He flicked his hair. His bicep flexed. My heart fluttered.

What was happening to me? Without thinking, I got to my feet.

"Are you OK?" Dwayne leaned over and gripped my arm before I could run out of the bar.

"Uh, yeah. Fine. I just, um, need to go to the bathroom." I shrugged his arm off and wove my way through the tables to find the restroom full with one man waiting outside.

What in the holy gay fuckety fuck was happening?

I gave the waiting man the obligatory *'sup?* chin salute, then leaned against the wall and stared at my shoes, praying I wouldn't break out in a cold sweat.

"Oh hey. Michael, right?" I looked up to find Jason standing in front of me.

Fuckety fucking fuckery!

I tried to smile. "Hey. Uh, yeah. Michael. That's me." Why was English suddenly my second language?

He grinned. "What did you think? I did the Lake Travis song a little different tonight."

"Yeah, I noticed." Had I noticed? I mean, I was practically daydreaming about offering him therapy throughout the song, but had I noticed it differed from the last time I'd heard it? "I really liked tonight better. I could feel it more."

He cocked his head, paused, then smiled. "Awesome. Thanks."

Before I knew what had happened, the dude in the bath-room exited and Jason snuck in, leaving the *'sup* guy and me staring at the locked bathroom door.

9

───────

Dwayne called Sunday morning and badgered me into brunch. I was sleeping in like a champ, but he sounded like a Catholic schoolgirl in trouble, so I knew I had to go.

Around eleven o'clock, I pulled up to our diner to find Dwayne pacing just outside the door. Was he muttering to himself while he paced? Oh, this was going to be juicy.

He saw me walking up and turned toward the door. Without a word, he opened it, went inside and plopped down at a table he'd already secured from Katie, our regular waitress. She gave me a look, something between sympathy and curiosity. A strange tingle tickled the back of my neck as I scooched into the booth and grabbed the creamer to doctor the mug of coffee Dwayne had thoughtfully ordered.

The cream had barely struck the surface when Dwayne's words tumbled out. "So, I met this guy last night. You know, I told you about him. Jim, the cute one from work. We talked after Jason's show, and he asked me to meet him at a bar."

He paused to gauge my reaction. I simply moved from creamer to sugar and raised an eyebrow.

"We met at the Chute."

My brow quirked in confusion at this new place I didn't recognize. Was this supposed to mean something?

"It's a small bar. We haven't been there. Well, you haven't been there. I've been there a million times. It's nice, mostly smoke-free, and has a small drag bar attached to a sporty bar. I like it. Anyway. You're getting me sidetracked."

Wow. Dwayne was babbling. I'd never seen this before. I sipped my coffee and grinned over the rim, enjoying the show. We might get a full-on meltdown today. Maybe Katie could bring me popcorn. Hell, she'd probably throw herself down and munch with me if the show had enough fireworks.

"Are you listening to me?"

I nodded my bleary head and took another sip. "Sorry. Go on. Cute Jim. The Chute. I'm with you."

"Anyway." He was *so* edgy. "We met at the Chute. I said that, didn't I? He had on these tight jeans and a stringy tank top. I'd never seen him wear anything but his uniform at work. Michael, he took my breath away. He was beautiful. I mean, *seriously* beautiful." He took a breath and gulped from his water glass. The ice rattled as his hand shook slightly.

"He's twenty-two, right?" I asked, more to confirm in his mind than mine. Dwayne was old enough to be the kid's father. This couldn't end well, and I was starting to get worried my friend was smitten.

"Michael, I'm totally smitten."

Oh shit.

"We got there around midnight and talked until they kicked us out at two. Then we went back to my place and talked for another three hours. I don't think I've ever talked to anyone that long, definitely not in our first real conversation. It flowed so easily."

The diner gods must've been watching, because Katie showed up in that moment, forcing Dwayne to stop rattling and breathe. She looked at him, then gave me a questioning look. I shrugged and chuckled, then mouthed "popcorn." She nearly dropped her order pad as a cackle burst out.

Dwayne looked up, and she covered her mouth with her pad. "Whatcha gonna have today, sweetie?" she asked Dwayne.

He gave me a snarky look, then turned back and ordered. I got my usual, wholegrain pancakes with a side of bacon and two over-medium eggs. She actually just told me that was my order, and I nodded. We're regulars, what can I say?

"Dwayne might need a side of chicken today. Seems he's been in the mood for it lately."

He wadded up a napkin and threw it at me as I spat coffee back into my cup. Katie cackled again and shuffled away, her head shaking the whole time.

"He sucked me off."

I nearly dropped my mug. Coffee splashed across the table and all over my white shirt. Katie was there in a flash with a bottle of soda water. Bless you, Katie.

"Did I hear you right? The staff diddled your staff?"

He gave me a sheepish grin and nodded. This forty-one-year-old man was *embarrassed*. I had to admit, it was kind of cute to see.

I grinned. "And? You know you can't just cum and run. I want details."

He huffed as if I was putting him out, then smiled.

"Oh … my … God. It was incredible, and I didn't see it coming."

I giggled like a schoolboy who'd heard a fart joke. He tossed another wadded napkin.

"Oh stop. We'd talked for so long that I'd lost track of time. I guess it was around three or four in the morning when he turned to me and, totally out of the blue, asked, 'Can I see your cock?' I was half-asleep until he asked that. I might never sleep again."

Our food arrived and Dwayne awkwardly changed the subject to football, of all topics. Katie nudged me with her arm and giggled. You can't fool a diner waitress.

Dwayne talked for another twenty minutes about the intricacies of a blow job from a twentysomething. He was usually even-keeled and focused on everyone else. It was fun to see him so excited and happy. He deserved it.

Katie brought the check and joked around with us a little, then we shuffled toward the door. Dwayne's nervous energy was spent—apparently for the *second* time in only a few hours. He turned the tables as I started toward my car. "So, what did you think of Jason last night?"

"Jason?" The sudden change in topic surprised me. "He's a good singer. Crowd seemed to like him."

He eyed me. There was a twist to his grin. "Mm-hmm."

"What?"

"I saw you two talking by the bathroom. He was leaning awfully close, and you seemed a little nervous and flushed when you got back to the table."

He didn't miss a damn thing.

I tried to laugh it off. "He just wanted to skip me and the

other guy in line for the bathroom. You know Jason, he's a
shameless flirt when he wants something."

He nodded and grunted in agreement. "Alright. I won't
press, but you two are my closest friends. If there's something
going on, I want to know about it."

"Yes, Dad."

He smacked my arm and shoved me into my car.

As I drove home, I thought back to how boyishly happy
Dwayne had been describing his close encounter of the
chicken kind. For the uninitiated, in gay vernacular, a chicken
is a young guy. That would make my dear Dwane a chicken
hawk—and if reports from last night were correct, he was a
lecherous one.

I was proud.

Then, for no apparent reason, Jason's face popped into my
head. I could see every strand of murky brown hair as it fell
across his forehead. He'd push it back, feigning annoyance,
but knowing that simple act drove the rest of us crazy. I
wondered what it would be like to reach up and push those
locks out of the way. A shiver worked its way into my chest.

What was I thinking? Jason was Dwayne's oldest friend—
and he was an aspiring singer in Nashville. 'Rudderless ship'
barely did him justice. I couldn't be interest in *him*—could I?

I tried to shake him out of my mind, but his stupid, perfect,
pearly-white smile kept flashing back to the fore. It was the
same smile that distracted pretty much everybody at the gym.
How could anyone have such flawless teeth? And how did he

get them to do that twinkle thing I was sure had to be animated, like in toothpaste commercials?

My car somehow found itself parking in the gym's lot. I'd packed a bag, swearing to make good use of my free Sunday afternoon. The gym was usually pretty empty on weekends, and I'd planned to get a great workout in. Then I looked up and realized Jason's car was parked opposite mine, its grille mimicking its owner's annoyingly angelic smile.

Focus, Michael. You're here to work out. Jason never pays attention to you anyway. Just go in, endure the pain, and go home. There's no need to even think about him and his hair-flicking madness.

So I told myself.

Five minutes into my workout, I looked up from the bench press to see Mr. Pearly Whites looming.

"Don't stop. I've got you." His hands gripped the pole … I mean, bar. The whole thing slammed loudly into the rack.

"Aw, you had more in you. Take a break and I'll push you all the way when I come back." Jason bounded across the gym floor to work his triceps.

Was every word out of his mouth sexual, or had Dwayne planted a seed that refused to be ignored? It sure was trying to take root and grow, or whatever seeds do when they're all about rolling in the hay with a hot guy. I watched Jason as he pulled the rope down and his triceps flexed to their limit. Despite the blasting air conditioner, he was dripping with sweat; it was soaking through his yellow tank top. I watched a bead fall from somewhere and trail into the crevice of his straining triceps. That might've been the hottest non-sexual thing I'd ever seen. I had to leave the bench for fear my own bar might distract others. It was standing at attention.

I got a drink from the water fountain near the locker rooms, as far from Jason as possible. The walk did me good and allowed Little Michael to droop back into place. It probably would've helped if I'd worn underwear and he wasn't tickled by silky fabric every time I moved, but I hated underwear—always had.

"You can't get away that easy. Back to the bench."

Shit. He was standing behind me. I could smell him, he was *that* close. Little Michael was intrigued and decided to look up again. This was going to be awkward.

"On my way, coach. One more drink," I said, buying time to get my shit back together.

He pressed against me and flames burst across my skin. He whispered in my ear, "I'm waiting. Come lift for me." I couldn't tell if his voice was sensual or playful, but it didn't matter. I was swooning.

I had the presence of mind to take another sip and free my personal space from his—though it was the last thing I *actually* wanted in that moment.

By some miracle of the gods, I managed to get through my final two sets of flat bench without busting a nut all over the gym. Little Michael behaved—sort of—and I don't think Jason ever saw how much he'd affected either of us. I stood and toweled the sweat off my arms, then turned toward the locker room. A familiar voice stopped me cold. "Oh no you don't. You have incline, decline and abs to do. Don't make me follow you around."

I couldn't decide whether to be annoyed he was making me work out more, thrilled he might follow me around—or *terrified* he might follow me around. The whole nut-busting thing was a real possibility if I had a Jason shadow all afternoon. Then again, there were worse ways to work out than looking up into dreamy eyes and a firm, muscular chest.

Stop it! There went Little Michael again, a dutiful soldier standing at attention. Ugh!

Thanks to Coach Jason barking "you got this" every two seconds, I pushed myself harder than I ever had at the gym. It felt good. No, it felt *amazing*. I had that pump-high that only comes after an intense workout. Add the Jason-high that came from being close to him for nearly an hour, and I was just plain high.

Now, stop that—not *that* kind of high. At that point in my pious, preacher's kid life, I'd never done any of that.

This was a wholesome, muscle-burn, boy-crush giddiness that coursed through my sore muscles. As I wobbled out the door, Jason chuckled and flashed every molar, canine, and whatever those other teeth are. I was too sore to swoon, but my insides did backflips.

Can your insides *do* backflips? Anyway.

He really was stunning. And the boy could sing. Damn.

I caught myself drumming my steering wheel and singing along with *Macarena* in the car as Betty drove me home. It had been a really good day.

10

The next day I worked on reports for my dad. I still worked for him in his wholesale drug business, but was less inclined to spend eternity on the road each week. My job had shifted into the back-office management of the business. Sounds pretty sexy, doesn't it? Don't be fooled. I created paperwork, entered the data that people wrote on that paperwork, then followed whatever instructions were left on the paperwork. It was mind-numbing, but I had no idea what I wanted to do with my life, and it was a job.

That afternoon, I left, packed bag in hand, to drive across town to referee a pair of high school preseason basketball games. That's right, yours truly was a basketball referee. Once the season heated up, I'd don stripes five or six nights each week. I'd even been accepted into a couple NAIA and JUCO conferences, which meant I got to drive a little farther and work college games.

When I was younger, I played YMCA basketball, but was never dedicated enough to get good. The high school I attended competed for state championship hardware every year, so making that team was a pipe dream. When I got into college, I still wanted to be on the court, and the guys and gals in stripes won me over. I got to be close to the action and get some great exercise. It was love at first whistle. Tweet? Blow?

Never mind.

Yes, it was a weird hobby where people constantly yelled at you and called you names that didn't make sense half the time—but any ref worth their stripes learned to tune all that out. There was always one mom hidden midway up the stands whose voice carried over all the others. You couldn't tune *her* out, but she usually yelled funny things we'd laugh about back in the locker room. I lost track of the times my partners or I would start a conversation at halftime with, "Did you hear what mom called you?" We'd all laugh at her creativity. Sometimes her name-calling stuck and a ref would earn a nickname that carried throughout his career, like Mav in *Top Gun*, but without the fighter jets or half-naked volleyball.

Mostly, I loved the game and being part of it. Working college games was a rush and a totally different level of professionalism and pressure. Coaches' jobs and kids' scholarships were on the line. The higher the level, the more money and prestige was at stake for the college or university too, but the rush was worth it. The play was a lot better, and there was an intensity to the game that lower levels just couldn't recreate.

I loved every minute on court.

And the exercise was amazing. They put a pedometer on a referee once and found he ran, on average, four to six miles per high school game and eight miles per college game. Multiply that by five to six nights of reffing, and Holy Roadrunner, Batman, that's a lot of miles!

I could eat *anything* and never gain weight. I know, most people would kill for that problem, but it drove me nuts because it made adding muscle painfully slow. Somehow, I still managed to grow. Between Peter and Jason punishing me daily at the gym, I started filling out my stripes, and even got called "pretty boy" a few times by wayward spectators. I knew it was meant to be insulting, but it made me smile the rest of the night.

Someone thought *I* was pretty. That blew my mind.

Monday night I worked a college preseason scrimmage, then a pair of high school games Tuesday evening. Wednesday was blessedly free of basketball, so I wrapped work early, determined to get a good workout in and relax in front of the TV. I stopped by the grocery store for a pre-workout snack.

The register ringer-upper cocked her head at the lonely apple that wobbled down the conveyor belt toward the scanner thingy. "That's it?" she asked.

I smiled and nodded, then counted out the change I knew would be exactly right. I did this routine almost every day. The apple gave me a quick boost of good sugars before my work-out, just enough to help me push through the pain and get a good pump. It made for a tasty, healthy snack, but also created a funny scene in the store. Great on so many levels.

When I pulled into the gym's parking lot, I was pleasantly surprised to spot a space by the front door. I gave Betty a jolt, determined to not lose my Princess Parking. As I pulled in, I got my second surprise. Jason's car was in the neighboring space.

Maybe Wednesdays were good days after all.

I couldn't suppress my grin as I pictured Jason rushing to the door to greet me. He'd throw his arms wide and wrap me in the same tight hug he gave Dwayne, but with the added thrill of a passionate kiss and open declaration of his undying affection.

It was a nice daydream.

I woke from it a second later and made my way through the door. The only person to greet me was the desk dude who scanned my badge. Jason was nowhere to be seen.

Oh well.

I took the long way through the machines, just to see if I could spot Jason working out somewhere. When that failed, I headed into the locker room and changed into my workout clothes. I'd been working out now for about six months and had finally become proud enough to switch from T-shirts to tank tops. That was a huge adjustment for the skinny kid, a little like jumping out of a perfectly good airplane that first time.

Nope, I've never done that, but this is a story. Use your imagination, for Pete's sake.

As I glanced in the mirror on the way back to the floor, I still couldn't believe *my* body was growing and changing. I looked athletic; I felt stronger. It was exhilarating. For the first time in my life, I wasn't a toothpick.

I was feeling pretty darn good about Wednesday when my shoes struck the familiar rubber mat of the weight room, and then I remembered it was leg day, and all the positive vibes drained away. Nobody in their right mind liked leg day. We worked legs because turning into 'tits on sticks' wasn't attractive, but I knew I'd be walking funny and burning painfully before it was all over.

While that might also describe the hours after Fly Boy did

his thing with his giant … silk ties, I can assure you, it's *not* the same pain.

Halfway through my fourth set of leg presses, Jason's upside-down face appeared as he hovered above and behind me. I must've been four shades of red and straining because he stifled a laugh that made me lose my concentration. The weights slammed back into place, sending my knees into my chest. Smooth, Michael. Real smooth.

"Nice set," he teased.

I tried to smile, but was still deciding whether life was worth it on leg day. "Thanks. I think."

"So, I have another performance tonight. It's at the Wildhorse, kind of a big deal. Can I count you in? I think Dwayne's going, so you'll know someone there."

Did Jason just ask me out? Did he want me there to support him—or did he *just want me there*? My heart skipped a beat. "Uh, sure. Sounds great. What time?"

"I don't go on until ten. Hope that's not too late. I know you work a regular job."

"Nah. That's fine. Looking forward to it." I started to stand, but my legs protested. Before I could brace myself, Jason said "thanks" and moved on. He bounced from one person to the next, no doubt drumming up a crowd. He had to do that. The more people who attended, the more times he'd be invited back to perform, and the more tips he'd make. Those other people were all part of the business of a starving artist.

His invitation to me was different. He'd singled me out. He wanted *me* there. Right there in the middle of the gym, surrounded by massive bodybuilders, I giggled. That earned a few odd glances, but I didn't care.

Wednesdays were suddenly awesome.

I'D NEVER BEEN TO THE WILDHORSE.

It was a massive, multi-story country bar owned by Gaylord, the folks who also owned the Grand Ole Opry and built the sprawling Opryland Hotel. They didn't know how to *do* small. The bottom floor was centered on a fenced-in wooden dance floor and was rarely without a few men and women struggling to grasp the basics of line dancing. The upstairs bars were largely focused on banister viewing of the downstairs, but there were quiet couches and other seating for those wishing an escape from country's finest. Fast-paced, twangy songs blasted throughout, causing even the most stoic barfly to bop his head or wiggle her shoulders.

The place felt alive from the moment I walked in.

I scanned the bars that wound around the edge of the place, looking for Dwayne, finally locating him in the corner, cradling a Jack and Coke with a gazillion limes. Another glass full of limes rested behind him on the bar. Backups, I assumed.

We settled onto our stools and I ordered a Coke, eliciting an eye roll from my gay godfather. "Where's Jason? And where will he sing? I don't see a stage or mic stand anywhere."

Dwayne pointed to the dance floor. "They'll set up a mic for him in the center of the floor. All the lights will drop and he'll be out there alone in a spotlight."

I shivered. "Sounds terrifying."

He laughed. "Jason will eat it up. He's never met a spot-light he didn't crave."

"He does look good in bright lights."

Dwayne shot me a look I couldn't interpret, then held it for a long moment. My skin crawled under his gaze. Had I said something wrong?

The lights flickered and staff worked to clear the dance floor so they could set up for the night's headliner. A buzz ran through the crowd. That was the first time I thought Jason might be kind of famous. He really wasn't. They did that for anyone who sang. Most of the people in the Wildhorse were tourists who didn't know a lounge singer from an Opry member—not that I was much better.

The lights dimmed and the spotlight flared, forming a stage out of a small circle of well-lit dance floor. One heart-beat, then two. Then Jason appeared and filled that stage of illumination. He was wearing tight jeans and a black cowboy-style shirt with white fringe. He flashed his trademark smile, and I swear his teeth glittered.

My heart fluttered.

I *felt* Dwayne staring at me from the side and turned to give him the universal 'What are you staring at?' shrug and brow raise. He shook his head and leaned toward me as Jason started singing. "He's not on the market," Dwayne whispered. "You know that, right?"

Now my racing heart tripped over its little arterial feet. How had Dwayne known I was crushing on him? I'd been *so* careful. My shock must've shown because he chuckled and shook his head again. "You've been mooning over him for weeks. How many times are you going to tell me what he wore to the gym? I think I know his wardrobe better than he does now."

My ears turned red. "I guess I have kinda talked about him. A little."

He snorted. "A little?" His eyes turned serious. "If I thought you had a shot with Jason, I'd be the first one telling you to go for it. The problem is that *nobody* has a shot with him. He's totally wrapped up in trying to make it in music and doesn't want anything that might be a distraction. There's been a line of men following him for years, but I can't remember the last time he actually went on a date."

My eyes fell. I loved having a friend who would be brutally honest, but hated his brutal honesty in that moment. "But he flirts with me at the gym. Like, *really* flirts."

"Michael, he would flirt with a rock if it could buy a ticket to one of his shows. I'm not trying to be cruel, but there's no hope there. Zero. It's better you realize that now than spend months—or longer—hoping for something that won't ever happen."

My eyes drifted back to the angel in his beam of light. His voice made me warm, and that smile … I didn't want to believe Dwayne, but replaying Jason's *flirting* at the gym made me question my confidence. He had left my side and continued his rounds to every person in the gym. He'd leaned over their machines—just as he had mine. He'd flashed the same smile, given the same intense gaze. He was a performer. It was *his job* to make people feel like they were the only person in the room when he spoke to them.

I wanted to be the only person in the room.

My heart finally settled into a slow, melancholy rhythm. Jason's songs were still amazing, but I struggled to keep my eyes on him as he delivered them. When I closed my eyes to escape, he was still there, smiling and making me feel things I didn't fully understand.

I couldn't escape him. I didn't want to.

Dwayne and I didn't talk much throughout the set. Jason finished, received raucous applause, then exited the stage to a waiting drink the bartender had made especially for the guest star of the evening. He didn't stop by or even glance in our direction.

I left the Wildhorse dejected.

Jason liked me. I *knew* it. He'd breathed on my neck while I did shoulder shrugs. Who did that? At least, who did that without liking the shoulder they're huffing on?

He *had* to like me.

Betty wandered aimlessly around downtown, partly because I didn't know where I wanted to go, and partly because I had the most atrocious sense of direction of any person alive. I could get lost pulling out of my own driveway. I definitely got lost that night.

When I finally found my bearings, it was around two in the morning. I was tired and sad. I wanted Jason to magically appear and tell me everything would be alright as he cradled me against his firm, muscular bosom.

Shit, I had it bad.

Without thinking, Betty found a familiar road. I recognized buildings and street signs. I pulled off to the side, into one of those parallel parking spaces that still confounded my driving skills, and rested my forehead against the steering wheel.

Footsteps jarred me out of my sad slumber. When I looked up, Jason had returned home and was walking from his car to his condo door.

Yes, I'd stalked my man-crush and was sitting outside his condo.

Give me *some* credit. I was parked discreetly across a little park that straddled his parking lot, not actually *in* the lot. The distinction might not sound like much to you, but to me it was the difference between a star-crossed lover and some psycho stalker. I was desperate to stay on the good side of that line, even though I knew I was dangerously close to crossing it.

Jason disappeared inside.

I needed air, so I did the smartest thing I could think of. I got out of my car and walked around the grassy park.

No, that *wasn't* very smart. It was precisely what a stalker would do as he bought time before sneaking inside to dismember his prey. I wanted Jason's member to remain intact. I had uses for his member. Dreams about it, actually. Dreams with condiments, or not.

Too much?

Anyway. Betty glared accusingly from her space by the park, and I finally drove my sorry, sad ass home.

Wednesdays sucked.

11

"You ended up where?" Dwayne bristled as he spoke. I'd never seen him upset or angry, but the color rising across his neck told me I was about to learn what his wrath was like. I shrank in my seat.

"I didn't go to his condo, just the park across from it."

"Michael, seriously?" He set his lime-laden drink down a little too hard, and poor Jack spilled all over the bar. "This isn't good. Not good at all. You can't turn into *that* kind of person. Do you hear me? What were you thinking?"

The preacher's kid in me knew exactly what I *should* be thinking, what I *should* be feeling. Guilt. That was the go-to. When all else failed, feel guilty. I was good at that.

So, I did.

"I'm sorry," my small voice answered. "I just wanted to see him again."

"That's no excuse. Promise me you'll never do anything like that again."

I looked up and found the most peaceful man I'd ever met

glaring at me as though I'd run his mother down with my car. I wanted to crawl under the bar. "I promise," I squeaked.

Dwayne stood there and stared like a disappointed parent whose child had stolen a candy bar from their favorite local store—hands on his hips, brows furrowed, scowling mouth. He had the look perfectly set.

I couldn't meet his eyes.

Cowboy Rick wandered over and stepped in between us—well, as best he could from across the bar. He was like a boxing referee trying to break up two fighters from outside the ring. He leaned over.

"You guys alright? Dwayne, you need another?" He wiped up the spilled drink and swept the glass away.

Dwayne nodded but didn't speak, then the air whistled out of his balloon and he sat beside me. I felt his hand press against my shoulder.

"Michael, you're important to me. I really care about you. I want you to be happy." He sucked in a breath, seemingly buying himself time to measure his words. "I know last night wasn't who you are, and I also know you've got a big crush on a very unattainable boy. You have to let that go. Just trust me here, OK?"

I was so ashamed. Worse, I felt like I'd disappointed Dwayne.

I didn't trust myself to speak, so I just nodded.

12

———————

Acouple weeks passed. Most days were spent in utter boredom doing random tasks for my dad's business. Basketball season was entering the busy period, so I donned stripes most nights. On the few when I didn't have to referee, I followed my routine as if it were a religion: leave work at four-thirty, stop at the store for my pre-workout apple, work out, go home. Rinse and repeat.

Dwayne and I met up for lunch a couple times, but never talked about anything more substantial than the latest boy making his ankle bracelet buzz. I joked about getting a button I could use to make the imaginary device vibrate just to watch him twitch. That usually earned a halfhearted slap on the arm, but it was funny. Dwayne could always bring a smile to my face.

I tried not to think about Jason. That was easier said than done.

I'd never been in love before—and I didn't even know if this qualified for that lofty category, but I was definitely in *something*—in over my head, most likely.

Dwayne prodded a few times, ensuring my psycho-stalking proclivity hadn't returned. It hadn't. I was a smitten puppy, but one that took well to training. Daddy Dwayne said don't go there, so I didn't. Although, I *really* wanted to, even just to see Jason walk from his car to his door. His butt puckered as he walked. It was hot.

Ugh. I had to get a life.

I went straight from work to my high school basketball assignment. Officiating always made me feel better. Between the exercise and the intense focus it required, being on court was an escape from everyday problems, such as pining after some unattainable singer with wavy hair and sparkling teeth.

I got home around ten thirty, ate a snack, and tossed myself on the couch. Once again, the television programming gods had taken the lazy route and every channel was showing reruns of some show I didn't care about. I tried watching the news, but that was depressing.

Peter bounced into the room with his perpetually annoying well of bubbling energy. "I'm going out with the gang. Want to come?"

That meant he was going to a straight bar, probably a sports bar, with four girls who would preen and fawn over him all night. Yes, it was *exactly* as exciting as it sounded, especially to the guy who wouldn't be the object of any of the aforementioned fawning.

"Nah. I'm beat, might even turn in early," I said.

He finished lacing up his shoes. "Suit yourself, old man. It's Friday night and you're young. You need to get out more. Who knows? One of the girls tonight might actually like nerdy old men." He jabbed me good-naturedly with his elbow.

Yes, I knew I needed to tell him about the whole *liking*

boys thing. A pang of guilt shot through me as I heard the door slam behind him. Peter was such a good guy, and an even better roommate. He deserved the truth—but I hadn't admitted *that* truth to myself yet. How was I supposed to say it out loud to someone else?

I flung my head into the fluffy comfort of our couch and stared at the ceiling, barely hearing the weatherman babbling about rain coming this weekend.

Maybe Peter was right. Maybe I should get out of the house and pull my mind out of my Jason-induced funk. I turned the TV off, wandered into my room, threw on some jeans and the cleanest shirt I could find, then headed out. The Connection was calling. This time, I swore I would stay long enough to actually experience the place—unless Fly Boy happened to be there again. I'd definitely leave early for another round of tie-your-partner.

Thirty minutes and three wrong turns later, I pulled into the parking lot. It was packed; cars were lined up halfway down the street. It had been full that first night Dwayne tricked me into going to a gay bar, but nothing like this. For some reason, butterflies were banging around inside my chest. I watched the guys laughing and hugging as they met each other in the line or ran into friends in the parking lot. The mood was festive.

Why was I suddenly nervous? Hadn't my two past visits been positive experiences, ending in happy … never mind.

A group of five incredibly fit guys in tight T-shirts strutted by. One of them craned his neck to get a look at me after they'd passed. He gave me a sexy grin and a wink.

This was *exactly* what I needed.

———

IT TOOK TEN MINUTES TO FIND A PARKING SPACE, WAIT IN LINE, and wade through the sardine can of an entrance. I turned into the country bar out of habit, as if a third visit could produce a habit. Cowboy Rick and two other bartenders were slinging drinks faster than Julia Childs chopping potatoes. For the heathens among us who don't get that reference, that means *really* fast. Think Ginsu knife fast.

I think I'm hungry. Anyway.

I got halfway through the throng before Rick looked up and saw me. I was surprised when he smiled broadly and waved me up to the bar, never missing a beat in his order-taking and drink-mixing. He was a true pro.

He craned across the bar and gave me a warm hug when I got close enough. I hadn't experienced the universal gay version of two kisses on either cheek, so my return squeeze was a little awkward. An old guy standing by, quietly sipping something fruity, grinned at my discomfort.

"You missed the past few weeks. Michael, right?" Rick really didn't miss a beat.

"Yeah, Dwayne dragged me to other places."

He looked around me. "Where is the old coot? I haven't seen him tonight."

I laughed. Anyone who made fun of Dwayne the same way I did had to be alright. "He's working late. I doubt he'll be out tonight. You know, being old and all."

Rick laughed as he shook a margarita. The old guy next to me scowled. Guess Grandpa didn't appreciate the jokes of young folk.

I turned to start scanning the crowd when a thunk drew me

back to the bar. "On me. It's good to see you again." Rick winked and blew me an air kiss. "Can't chat. Busy, busy." He darted away to take another order.

I looked down to find a Coke with three limes stuffed on the rim, his little homage to our missing Dwayne. Cautiously, I sipped, wondering if he'd actually given me Dwayne's Drink-o-Death. Nope. Plain ol' Coke.

Damn, he was good.

Drink in hand, I wedged my way through the pack to get some air on the normally quiet outdoor patio. It, too, was packed, but the cooler air felt almost as good as the lack of cigarette smoke smelled. I hated that stuff.

The price we pay for a night of gay. Hey, I made a funny.

I laughed at my own silliness and took another sip, then wandered back inside and watched the line dancers do their thing. The floor was filled, as four full lines of dancers wiggled and kicked to fast-paced music. I was mesmerized. They danced through six full songs before I realized how long I'd been standing there. Each song had its own footwork, and the pack of men knew every move. How was that possible? The DJ wasn't playing a rehearsed set, yet they could *name that tune* in three notes—mostly with their feet. It was impressive.

My country music tolerance was exceeded by the sixth song, so I decided to visit the main floor.

Holy Mary and Joseph … and their dogs … and cats … and pet fish.

There was music and flashing lights, but absolutely no dancing. It wasn't possible. Overheated bodies were packed in so tight there was no hope of even a bad white-man dance, much less the more exotic kind I'd witnessed on the boxes a month ago. The mass of men just swayed, like one large organism under a microscope wobbling back and forth to the rhythm.

What surprised me the most was that no one seemed to care about their arms being pinned to their sides by the wall of half-naked, sweaty bodies. Come to think of it, that might've been the whole point of being there.

Little Michael found room to dance as the pack of muscular men who'd passed while I was parking moved in around me. The Winker handed his drink to a buddy then turned to face me. There was no avoiding his chest pressing into mine as the amoeba swayed toward my side of the floor. That sent a thrill up my spine. I looked up and he was smiling, his eyes locking on mine. One of his hands teased my arm, starting with my wrist and slowly tracing a path up to my shoulder. His fingertips barely touched the hairs on my arms, lighting my skin on fire as they passed. When I shivered, his grin broadened.

I was frozen. Little Michael wasn't. Winker's other hand pressed into him and his eyes widened in a smile that matched the one parting his mouth. There was more than amusement in his gaze. There was hunger.

Damn, I was hungry too.

He leaned forward and pressed a soft kiss on my lips, then leaned his mouth to my ear. "Find me later. I'm Thomas."

I tried to breathe. His warm breath clung to the skin of my neck, and I watched as he and his friends vanished into the crowd. He looked back once and winked again.

The sound of applause shook me out of my stare. I turned toward the noise to find two young guys giggling and clapping. One of them called out, "Honey, you tease those boys." Another round of giggles ensued and they drifted away.

When did *I* do any teasing? I was the unsuspecting, innocent teasee in this situation—not that I was complaining.

I'd never had much confidence, and here I was being approached by darn hot men. Not approached—kissed and rubbed and teased. They wanted to tease *me*. The butterflies had to move aside because a wave of newfound pride swelled my recently worked-out pecs. I threw my head up, chest out, and strutted my way through the crowd. My butt was squeezed three separate times during that strut. Anywhere else, we might be calling the police. In that bar, my puffiness grew with every grab. They were grabbing *my* butt! I was a butt-grab-bable gay—

Guy. I meant, butt-grabbable *guy*.

I still wasn't G.

I couldn't be *that*.

13

———————

T he next night, I couldn't wait for midnight and another
visit to the Connection. According to Cowboy Rick,
Saturdays were busier than Fridays. I had a hard time
believing they could fit in any more people than I'd seen the
night before, but Oracle Rick proved himself omniscient.

Holy gays on a stick, it was even more crowded than
before. The line to get in was nearly to the street—not the
cars, the people queuing out front.

I was giddy.

Committed to my ritual, I visited Rick, got my *on me*
Coke, watched some line dancing, then headed to the main
floor. Michael must follow routine.

After my third lap around the dance floor—and two
glorious butt squeezes—I decided to head to my original
hiding space in the corner. I needed a break, and it would be
nice to just watch and breathe without so many bodies
pressing against me. When I got to that side of the bar, I was
annoyed to find someone standing in my spot. How dare he?
Didn't he know that was where I lurked in the darkness?

Then I looked a little closer. Oh, this one was hot. Maybe he *could* stand in my spot, after all.

He was tall, maybe six three, with short brown hair. The disco lights flashing in the darkness made it impossible to tell much more than that, but his white T-shirt glowed luminescent. I *could* see a massive chest poking through strained fabric. Little Michael loved some big chesticles. He let me know it too.

I stood three guys over from White Shirt for two songs, sneaking peeks when I thought he wasn't looking.

Holy Massive Man Boobs.

Halfway through the fourth song, I was actually watching someone else as they climbed atop a box when a voice startled me. "You've been watching me."

I jumped as I turned and found myself eye-level with delicious, hard, erect nipples—I mean White Shirt.

His nipples *were* erect.

But fear not, I was smooth. "I, uh, what? No. I wasn't. I mean, kind of. But not really. I wouldn't—"

He laughed and cocked his head, studying me quietly. His eyes twinkled in the flashes of light. "You're cute," he said with a smile.

I was completely befuzzled now. "Thanks. Um, you have big boobs. Ugh, I mean chest. You have a nice chest. It's big and hard. *Your chest*, I mean. Oh, never mind."

The brilliance of my reddened face had surely lit up the darkness, and I turned to seek the fastest exit.

His hand cupped my cheek before I could. He guided my face, urging my eyes back to his. "Thank you."

I had just verbally thrown up on my shoes and all he said was, 'Thank you?' What the actual fuck?

"I'm Carter."

Finally, something I couldn't screw up. "I'm Jason—I mean, Michael. I'm Michael."

"Who's Jason?"

"Not me. I'm not him. He's not me. I mean … I'm Michael."

Had someone struck my head rather than squeezed my ass? What was happening? I swear I'm a smart, well-spoken guy, but in that moment, English was *definitely* my second language.

He chuckled. "Would you like to go into the show bar? They won't start for another thirty minutes, and it'll be easier to talk without all this." He waved his hand at the amoeba.

I nodded, afraid to open my mouth and let stupid fall out again, then followed as he shoved his way into the open space of the show bar.

The lights were still bright—well, as bright as bar lights got before closing—and I could see Carter more clearly. His eyes were a light hazel, made even lighter by the black-light effect of his white shirt. He had a strong jaw and chiseled features that matched the impressive chest my eyes couldn't stay away from.

As he started to speak, his lips commanded my attention— and not for the reason you're thinking, you dirty possum. They formed an incredibly thin line, almost as if no lips existed, only an opening through which he spoke. When his mouth was closed, a tiny speed bump surfaced, giving the impression he was smirking even when he wasn't. It was odd and unlike any lips I'd seen before, but kind of cute in a malformed-Ken-doll's-missing-penis sort of way.

They were different, but definitely didn't make him less hot.

"This is much better. I can actually hear you in here." He held up an empty plastic cup. "I need a refill. What are you having?"

I raised my empty cocktail glass. "Just Coke."

His lips quirked. Twerked. Pursed. I really didn't know what to call it. "*Just* Coke? You're not drinking?"

I shook my head. "Alcohol makes me sleepy. Coke is good."

He chuckled and shrugged. When he returned, he handed me a plastic cup filled with fizzy goodness. There were three limes on the rim. "The bartender said you needed those. I've learned not to question the staff here."

I looked up and was shocked to find a bartender I didn't know. He grinned and waved. Apparently, the Gay Force was strong with this one.

"You come here a lot?" he asked, staring at the limes.

I shook my head mid-sip. "This is just my third time."

He gave the lime a last glare, then looked out toward the stage. "Yeah. I don't mind the bars, I guess, but they're not my favorite. All the smoke drives my sinuses crazy, and half the guys are just looking to get laid."

The little voice in my head spoke. *Guilty as charged, Your Honor.* I licked his chest with my eyes again. *Seriously guilty, sir.*

My normal voice said, "Yeah, I know what you mean. I hate how my jeans smell like smoke even after I wash them."

He quirked his head and smiled, studying me again. It wasn't the *come fuck me* look I'd gotten from Winker the night before, though I wasn't complaining about that. No, his gaze was earnest, curious, intrigued. I think he wanted to learn about me, not just get me naked.

This was different.

Over the next thirty minutes, I learned that Carter was an executive for a shoe company. He did numbers or stats or something. He spoke in precise, clipped phrases when talking about work, and I got the impression he was a muckety-muck of some sort. My eyes glazed as he described inventory and the inner workings of the footwear business. He'd been with the same company for more than fifteen years and was very proud to have built a 401(k) in the high five figures. I'd have to remember to find out what a 401(k) was later.

He'd been married for a few years and had two small children.

Huh. How did that work for a gay man?

He explained that he'd met his ex-wife in college, and they'd done what was expected. He'd known he was attracted to men, but didn't know any gays and thought *it* would just go away when he got married. He'd joined a church with his wife and had two kids trying to make *it* go away.

It never went away.

Now he was divorced with shared custody. His wife was as good with him being gay as a woman could be. She'd been hurt, wanted to know what she'd done *to turn him*, but in the end loved him enough to want Carter to live a happy life without hiding his true self.

I'd lost track of time when men started filling up the seating. It was getting harder to hear each other.

"Looks like the show is about to start," he said.

I looked around and nodded.

"Do you like drag?" he asked.

I'd never really thought about it. I shrugged. "I guess it's OK. Wearing women's clothes isn't my thing, but if someone else wants to do it, why not?"

He rolled his eyes and chuckled. "I need another drink before this starts. Want one? Still Coke?"

"Sure. Thanks."

He reached out, gripped my shoulder gently and held it a second, then turned to walk to the bar.

This was the strangest bar meeting ever. He was such a nice guy, and genuinely wanted to know about me, who I was, what I liked, what made me happy. In my vast experience of three visits to the bar, no one had wanted to get to know *me*, only Little Michael.

Again, not judging. Little Michael enjoyed the attention; *craved* it, actually. My sheltered youth among the wolf pack cried out for him to get more action.

But there was something about Carter, about this conversation, how he looked at me … I don't know. It was new and somehow *more*. It didn't make me want to strip down and hump like Winker had, but it brought a smile to my face. A strange warmth I didn't recognize flowed in my chest.

A moment later, Carter returned with the promised refill. Our fingers touched as he handed me my Coke, and I let them linger a second before securing the plastic cup. There it was again, that warmth.

We watched three songs' worth of drag before reaching a mutual point of boredom. Don't get me wrong, the drag queens in Nashville were world class, with their massive wigs and even bigger boobs. They probably spent hours squeezing into their heavily sequined gowns. I didn't want to know how much makeup they puttied on before entering the stage—it was Tammy Faye thick. Beyond their appearance, the queens were incredible performers, as comfortable on stage as anyone you might see in Vegas. Sure, most of them lip-synched to the music, but they were on point with it. There were even a few who sang, and their voices were Nashville-starving-artist impressive.

So when I say we reached our tipping point, it wasn't out of disrespect for the quality of the entertainment. Drag just wasn't a passion for either of us, as it appeared to be for the enthusiastic fans currently screaming and waving dollar bills from the front row. They *really* loved men in dresses.

We walked back toward the dance bar and Carter paused, then he committed one of the most grievous gay-bar sins imaginable. He yawned. And not one of those tiny covered-by-the-back-of-one's-hand yawns. This was a full-throated, lay-your-head-back-and-belt-it-out yawn. He didn't even bother trying to cover his mouth, and I could hear the satisfied groan-like sound over the competing disco and drag music. He turned to me with an unapologetic look.

"I think it's time for me to go. My battery's getting low." He gave me a pursed smile, then leaned over and kissed my cheek. "I'd like to see you again, if you're up for it."

I guessed being shocked out of my mind was going to become a regular occurrence at the Connection. While my emotions throughout the night were generally less about forking than spooning, I still thought we'd end up hooking up. Wasn't that what all gays did when they went to a bar? It's practically a rule or something, right? Wasn't that why we paid a cover—to *guarantee* a lucky night? No one had given me a copy of the Gay Handbook yet, and I was sure it would be murky on this point.

I looked up at his sincere face and smushy, thin lips. He had kind eyes. With a quick nod, I said, "I'd really like that."

He grabbed my hand and led me to the long bar by the disco floor, then waved one of the five bartenders down. Five. Seriously. And they were never standing still or without a glass to fill. It was remarkable.

The hottie behind the bar gave Carter two business cards with the Connection's logo and phone number stamped on them. On the reverse side was a series of prompts for patrons to complete, like a questionnaire you fill out when starting a new job.

My name and number:

His name and number:

How I can remember him:

I actually laughed out loud as I read that last one. It made sense. In an ocean filled with pecs, lats, and triceps—and every other kind of exposed muscle—you might need a note to remember which guy had given which card.

Were we all *total* sluts?

Carter handed me his card without completing question three. I did the same, not wanting to presume his memory aid for him, though I got the impression he didn't give his number out often.

He leaned over, kissed my cheek tenderly one last time, then turned and made his way to the parking lot. I watched him until he disappeared. He towered over most of the guys. More than a few of them turned to admire his chest as he passed, and a spike of red-hot something seared through me. Was I jealous? I'd just met him. That was ridiculous. Then a guy reached up and touched his chest, and that spike turned into a Lorena Bobbitt stab—or was she more a cutter? Ew. Never mind.

When he was out of sight, I turned back to the bar and looked at the card he'd handed me, its neat cursive script like a warm smile. I grabbed the pen and wrote my memory aid in spot number three: *Big chest. Tiny lips. Shoe guy.*

14

Morning came annoyingly early the next day. Peter was his usually chipper self, blending some kind of terrible concoction that I supposed helped him extend the life of his ever-present abs.

I really hated his perfection, especially since he spent most of his in-apartment time without a shirt. He was just being comfortable and had no idea how *un*comfortable it made me.

God, he was beautiful.

Anyway. Stop distracting me.

I shuffled my bleary-headed butt to the counter and nearly fell asleep watching the blender spin.

"Late night?" he asked with a smirk.

I shrugged. "I guess. Got in around one thirty or so."

"Oh, so didn't get any ass?"

Ass? Oh shit. He'd never asked that before. What did he mean? Was he being literal? Did he suspect something?

Panic rushed through me and I broke into a cold sweat. We couldn't have *that* conversation now. Maybe never.

He grinned as I squirmed. "So you didn't meet any girls

worth mentioning? Thought so. Don't worry, we all strike out some nights."

Whew. I breathed again. Girls have asses too, right?

"Yeah, totally struck out. That's why I came home early."

Thank you, baby Jesus.

He downed his Titanic-sized glass of protein madness, then padded into his room to *finally* put on a shirt and head to the gym. Sundays were busy with his personal training clients, and I knew I wouldn't see him again before seven or so. On his way out, he gave me a good bro-tap on the shoulder. I tried not to wish it was more, but the little devil was getting louder every day. The angel must've been bound and gagged some-where in the recesses of my subconscious, probably with silk ties—I hadn't heard her voice in months.

Following Peter's example, I mindlessly prepared a healthy breakfast, of a cherry Pop Tart with icing and sprin-kles. Hey, stop laughing. Those things are a gift from the gods. All of them. The whole Mount Olympus gang granted humans a glorious inheritance when Pop Tarts were bequeathed upon us.

OK. Maybe they weren't *all* that, but they were tasty. Especially with a little melted butter.

As I stuffed the last crusty bite into my mouth, our ancient phone whirred and halted my chewing. Who would call at this hour? It was eleven o'clock in the morning on a Sunday. How rude!

"Hello?"

"Hi. Is this Michael?" I immediately recognized the voice. Images of hard, rounded pecs materialized in my mind, and I couldn't stop a reflexive smile.

"Hey, Carter."

There was a second of silence, then he said, "You recognized my voice?" I thought he sounded pleased and was teasing me a bit.

"We did talk for over an hour last night." I decided to tease back. "It's eleven o'clock the day after we met. Miss me already?"

He chuckled, and I could see his itty-bitty lips curling upward. "I wouldn't go *that* far, but I guess I was thinking about you this morning. Does that count?"

That warmth rushed to greet me again. I reveled in its touch. He *had* missed me. Holy cow … and chicken … and pig. Please, English, stay my primary language. "Oh sure. That counts. You *definitely* missed me." My heart thrilled at the adorable giggle I heard through the receiver. "So, what do you do when you miss a boy you just met?" I was getting a little brave, maybe even cocky. This was fun.

He cleared his throat. "Well, in my world, I invite him to dinner. I like to cook, and from the looks of his shoulders and arms poking through his shirt last night, he has to eat to keep growing."

I nearly passed out. He'd noticed *my* arms? A guy with pecs the size of Kansas had noticed *my* chicken wings? English abandoned me. "Yeah, well, uh, I do eat. I mean, I like to eat. And have to, you know, for working out. 'Cause I do. Work out, I mean. And eat."

What had been a giggle turned in to a deep, full-throated laugh. There wasn't a mirror in our living room, but I was surely as red as the sprinkles I'd just devoured. I sounded like a complete and utter babbling idiot.

But the gentleman on the other end of the phone didn't pounce. He didn't take advantage of my obvious discomfort.

He simply calmed himself and said, "Good. If you're OK coming to my place, I'd like to cook you dinner tonight. Say, six o'clock?"

"Six?" I said, as if I'd need to confirm with my social secretary or some silliness. "Sure, I think that'll work."

What a moron.

He gave me a second to grab a pen. The only paper I could find was the Connection card from last night, which was actually perfect. I'd have all his info in one place. I jotted down his address, then hung up the phone.

The second the receiver hit the cradle, I was up in front of the television doing the goofiest white-man happy dance you've ever seen, chicken wings flapping wildly in the breeze. I couldn't contain my excitement. It just came out.

The growing pile of laundry in the corner practically flagged me back down to earth. Shit. I had work to do if I was going to be halfway presentable in a room brighter than the Connection's black-lit dance floor.

Then it hit me. I was actually going on a date—a real, sit-and-eat-dinner date—*with a guy*. For some reason, that made me more nervous than any other interaction I'd had with a man. Fly Boy had tried to shove himself all the way up to my lungs, but the thought of having dinner with a nice guy made me want to run and vomit at the same time. What evil magic was this?

I needed serious help before facing Carter again, so I grabbed the phone and called the one person who would know what to do.

"Hey, Michael. What's up?" Dwayne's warm voice sounded through the receiver.

"Code Red! Or DEFCON One. Or whatever term you gays use when there's an emergency. I need a Dwayne lunch, stat!"

He laughed at my excitement and appalling use of terms I clearly didn't understand. "Sure. I'm not doing anything. See you at the diner in an hour?"

"Great. Thanks. Oh, and this is a good emergency. Great, actually. The best."

He was laughing as I hung up the phone.

I'm such a goofball.

15

———————

For the first time since we'd met, I beat Dwayne to the diner and was sitting at our usual table, iced tea half-empty, when he arrived. The startled expression on his face was quickly replaced by a broad smile. He was always happy to see me. What an amazing friend.

"Alright. I'm here. What's the emergency?" he asked as he slid into the booth.

"I met a guy last night."

He rolled his eyes. "Yeah, it was Saturday. What's new these days?"

"Dwayne, this one was different. We actually *talked*."

He barked a laugh. "You know that's actually allowed? In fact, I highly encourage it. Did you get his name before he banged you into last week?"

"Ha ha. His name is Carter. He's a shoe guy."

His brows quirked like two caterpillars humping above his nose. He needed to take a weed whacker to them soon or someone might revoke his gay card. "Shoe guy?" he asked.

"Yeah, exec for a shoe company. I think he's their CFO or

comptroller or something. I didn't totally understand, but he sounded like a big deal."

Katie appeared and plopped down beside me, playfully shoving me out of the way with her ample hips. "Scoot it, precious. How are my boys?"

She was perky today.

Dwayne chuckled at my discomfort. "We're great. We're celebrating. Michael actually *talked* to a boy last night."

She feigned being impressed with bulging eyes and her mouth shaped like a giant O. "Good for you, little one. Just be careful. Most men only want one thing."

Dwayne nearly fell out of the booth laughing. When he came up for air, his eyes were moist. "Oh, that's usually what the little one beside you is hunting for. We're celebrating him actually getting the guy's name and having a conversation that *didn't* involve exchanging fluids."

"Dwayne!" I was shocked and embarrassed. Was I really *that* slutty?

"Look, Slutisha."

"Slutisha?" Now it was Katie's turn to cry. She wrapped her arm around my shoulders and gave me a squeeze. "You have your fun. You're only young once. Just be careful, OK?"

Her transition from hilarity to motherly advice jarred me a bit. There was genuine concern in her eyes. "I will. Thanks."

She took our orders and extracted herself from the booth, then shook her head and giggled as she walked away. I could hear her mutter "Slutisha" between chuckles.

Over lunch, I babbled, giving Dwayne every detail from last night with Carter. He listened with his usual attentiveness, asking questions and chuckling when I told him about the bartender loading me up with limes.

"You've only been there three times and the staff are already taking care of you. That's Rick's doing."

I was dumbfounded. "Why? There are thousands of guys there on the weekend. Why would they do that for me?"

He shrugged. "Hanging out with Jason over the years, I've learned a little about the bar community. The staff, at least the ones who've been there for a few years, are like family. They see everything you can imagine—and probably stuff neither of us can imagine. They look out for each other and for those they like or care about."

I still didn't get it. "OK, but why me? I've only talked to Rick a few times, and I'd never even met the bartender in the show bar."

He smiled. "I'm part of the family, and they know you're important to me."

He didn't elaborate. I wanted to ask a dozen more questions because that didn't make any sense to my wolfy brain, but he threw cash on the table and stood. "I need to run some errands, and you have laundry to do." He paused, then gave me a conspiratorial grin. "Please, pick a shirt without holes. I know you haven't earned your gay card yet, but you have to do better than that on a date."

I looked down at the small tear just above my right pec. "Good call."

I ONLY MADE ONE WRONG TURN DRIVING TO CARTER'S HOUSE. It added five minutes to the trek, but I'd left much earlier than was necessary, determined to be on time for my first official date with a dude. I found his house, then drove past, stopping in front of a neighbor's home a few houses down. My palms were wet and the lone random napkin in the car was now soaked. Terror struck as I looked at my hair in the mirror. I tried to make it lay down, but more than one cow had licked it to death earlier in the day—and they hadn't even thanked me for the action. How rude.

Realizing nothing would help the hair situation, I took a few deep breaths to try to slow my pulse. Why couldn't I breathe? This was ridiculous. We'd already met and talked for an hour. Now we were having dinner. It was just dinner. I ate all the time. I knew how to do dinner without throwing up on my shoes. There was *nothing* to be jittery about.

The pep talk didn't work. I was about to pee myself right there on Betty's faux-leather seats.

Baby Jesus, please don't let me pee myself. I'm begging.

I parked in Carter's driveway and stared up at the modest, one-story ranch home. His yard sprawled for a good half-acre and was full of lush, well-tended grass. The iconic red and yellow of a Cozy Coupe peeking around the corner caught my eye, and I remembered he had two toddlers. For some reason, that made me even more nervous.

Lord, I was a mess.

The door opened and Carter appeared wearing a long blue apron. On it, a salt shaker was dueling with a pepper shaker, each combatant wielding a steak knife like a sword. It was cute and somehow fit what I knew of him perfectly.

He watched through the screen door, then stepped out and tilted his head to the side as he walked up to Betty's driver's-side door. I rolled down the window.

"You want to eat out here?" he asked, a smirk playing on his lips.

My head swiveled around Betty, as if taking him seriously. I was such an idiot. "Uh, no, sorry. I was just … never mind."

He chuckled as I finally got out of the car. He pulled the oven mitt I hadn't seen off one hand and gave me a hug and peck on the cheek. Holy shit, I piddled. Right there in his driveway, I felt myself piddle my jeans a little bit.

Baby Jesus, why do you hate me? I even begged.

Thankfully, he didn't seem to notice and I followed him inside.

Carter's house was tasteful and simple, as modest and functional as the outside. I couldn't believe how clean it was; I had flashbacks of the mounds of laundry and other unknown objects strewn about my apartment. He was like an adult or something.

I asked to use his restroom, and he pointed down a narrow hallway. I didn't really have to go anymore, but the piddle spot needed work. On the way, I passed a bedroom. A mound of toys rose out of a bin in the corner, and brightly colored sheets and comforters covered the beds. I wasn't up on kids' cartoons and didn't recognize the characters frolicking across the covers. The room was small, but cozy and bright. It felt happy.

The smell of dripping chicken fat made my stomach gurgle. Satisfied the error of my ways had been corrected, I washed my hands and hurried down the hall toward the kitchen. There was no formal dining room, but the breakfast nook held a round wooden table laden with platters and dishes. Either Carter ate way more food than I thought possible, or he had serious portion control problems. I really didn't care which was true. It smelled amazing.

He looked up from stirring and smiled. As I leaned in the doorway to watch him in action, he handed me a tall glass filled with fizzing liquid. The rim was so covered in limes I didn't have room to take a sip. He chuckled as he handed it to me, evidently proud of his little joke, then gave me another peck on the cheek.

Damn if I didn't piddle again. What was this boy doing to me?

I evacuated the doorway and sat quickly at the table to cover my new wet spot. It wasn't like I'd unloaded my bladder, but the tiny bloom was growing and I wanted to protect my dignity.

A moment later, he set the last of the steaming dishes on the table and joined me, a glass of white wine in hand.

"I hope you like baked chicken with Cajun spices. I tend to cook simple and healthy. It's more a lifestyle than a diet these days. When you get to my age, you have to watch it more."

"Your age?" I blurted out, immediately regretting it.

He didn't flinch. "Yep. I'm thirty-six."

Holy cow. He was *old*. I was on a date with an old guy. How was he so hot at that age?

He must've seen the questions spinning in my head. "You're what, twenty-two, three?"

I puffed my chest out. "Twenty-four. Turn twenty-five in March."

He grinned as his brows rose. "Happy early birthday. You're moving up a box."

I cocked my head, confused, and he grinned. "On forms and insurance. You know, the check boxes usually go in five-year increments. You're moving to a new bracket on paperwork. It's sort of a milestone."

He sounded so smart when he talked.

I'd never thought about any of that. I didn't own any insurance and didn't have a 401(k). Hell, I worked for my dad. I suddenly felt tiny and unaccomplished.

He placed a hand on my arm and squeezed. "Enjoy being young. Before long, you'll round down with birthdays rather than up."

We grinned at each other like fools and he gestured for me to tuck in. He didn't need to tell me twice; the spread looked incredible. I just hoped my brain remembered how to use cutlery and, you know, chew without spilling down my front. The last thing I wanted was to have him hand me one of his children's bibs. He asked about working with my dad, and I asked about his work, though it sounded terribly boring. When he talked about his kids, the whole room lit up. Cade was three and Christian was five. Cade was finally learning more words, making it easier to know what he wanted. Carter beamed as he told me Cade called him "Ba Ba," the three-year-old version of Christian's "Daddy."

Carter's cheeks formed little dimples when he smiled. I wanted to reach up and run my thumb over one, but resisted. They were adorable.

He was adorable. No, he was hot, despite his advanced age.

Things grew quiet after that, save for the clanging and scraping of knives and forks. The silence became awkward.

"You OK?" I asked. He met my eyes. I could tell he wanted to ask something, but was afraid to. "Ask me anything. I'm an open book."

He sucked in a breath, and a suddenly tiny voice asked, "Do you like kids?"

I watched him. He was so sincere, so open and honest. I could feel his heart seize as he asked that question. Tension hung in the air. As nervous as I had been earlier, it never crossed my mind that *he* might hold some secret angst too. Yet here it was. Laid on the table as plainly as the Cajun chicken.

I kept my eyes steady and firm. "I do. Like them more than adults most of the time."

The relief on his face was perhaps the most beautiful thing I'd ever seen. I knew in that moment that he loved Cade and Christian more than life itself, and finding someone to share that joy with was core to his own happiness.

I also understood that as warm and loving as Carter was, as much as his children filled his life with laughter, he was *lonely*. He didn't just want companionship, he craved it, but was terrified it would elude him.

How I saw all that in one glance, I couldn't explain, but it was there. It was written across his face, and I could feel it slamming into my every sense.

He finally spoke again. "I don't date a lot, but so many guys run the second they learn about Cade and Christian." His eyes fell to his plate as his head drooped.

My heart ached for him. I reached across and gripped his hand. "I'm not running, Carter. I'm right here."

WE SEEMED TO HAVE BROKEN THROUGH SOME ICY WALL I hadn't realized was there, because Carter relaxed and conversation flowed freely. We finally set our forks down, and I scanned the empty platters. We'd done serious damage, and it was delicious. Sure, it was meat with some spices, but Carter really knew his way around a chicken.

Stop snickering. Not *that* kind of chicken. Although, on

behalf of chickens everywhere, I hoped he knew his way around *that* kind too. It would come in handy should we ever get naked. Glancing at his chest again, I really wanted that to happen soon.

Anyway.

His eyes widened when I insisted on helping him wash and put away the dishes. He washed, and I dried. Our elbows bumped more often than the rag hitting the wet plates. We laughed and cut up like little boys. It was odd how such a simple domestic task could turn into something so endearing, but I caught him smiling at me several times when he thought I wasn't looking. I suspect he caught me doing the same a time or two.

The whole night felt good. No, it felt *comfortable*, like putting on an old pair of slippers you found in the back of the closet. They fit just right, and warmed you in ways no new pair ever could.

Was it bad I just compared Shoe Guy to slippers?

Carter suggested we watch a movie. Lord, was that the story of my life or what? Did all gay men use the 'let's watch a movie' thing to get into each other's pants? Flashes of my first date with Joseph played in my head. The more I thought about it, the more I liked the idea, and wondered if Carter would make a move once we hit the couch.

I don't remember what movie we picked, but there were no moves. Carter got a couple pillows from the kids' room and stretched out on his extra-wide sofa. He patted the cushion in front of him, and I took my seat. He chuckled, reached up and gripped my shoulders, then repositioned me so I was prone in front of him. He pulled me tight against his chest with one arm. I nearly piddled again as I felt his pecs pressing against my back and the corded muscles of his arms envelop me.

Once the movie started, and I realized we really were going to watch it, I settled in and let myself enjoy the comfort and safety of his strength. He was tall enough that I wedged perfectly under his chin. A few times, I felt him squeeze a little tighter and nuzzle his chin against my head.

We just fit.

As the credits began to roll, I stirred and began to sit up.

"Want a snack?" he asked from behind.

I turned to face him, my dirty little mind wondering if he meant what I was thinking by *snack*. "Sure," I said, leaving our options open.

He untangled himself and padded into the kitchen.

Damn it. He meant an actual snack. Oh well.

I followed and watched as he pulled out a tub of cottage cheese and two cans of fruit—you know, the mixed fruit in a can with the little cherries. He scooped out a healthy bowl of cottage cheese, then topped it with the fruit, dropped in a spoon, and handed it to me. He made himself a bowl and lifted his spoon in salute. "I eat this every night before bed," he said, bringing his first bite to his mouth.

I couldn't remember the last time I'd eaten cottage cheese. Mixed with the fruit, it was actually tasty.

Wait, he'd said 'before bed,' hadn't he? My heart skipped a beat between spoonfuls. I looked up to find him watching me intently. My heart leapt into high gear, and I had a little trouble swallowing my bite.

He reached up with a napkin and wiped my lip.

Holy shit. *He just wiped my lip.*

It was the sweetest thing anyone had ever done to me—I mean, *for* me. Stop snickering.

I swooned, but tried to cover it by taking another bite.

"I have to work tomorrow, but you're welcome to stay—if you want to." That last part sounded like it came more from Cade than Carter. Was he as nervous as I was? Was that possible?

I met his eyes and hesitated. He struggled to hold my gaze this time. No way! He *was* nervous.

I asked the first thing that popped into my head. "Will you hold me like you did on the couch?"

His eyes snapped to mine, all hesitation gone, and he smiled. "All night long."

16

"He held me *all night*, Dwayne. We slept in our underwear, and he never tried to do anything other than kiss me goodnight. I don't think I've ever felt so safe and at peace in my life." I took a bite of eggs. "You need to meet Carter. I want to know what you think. He seems too good to be true—and did I mention he has a *massive* chest?"

Dwayne laughed and dribbled a little coffee onto the table. "Yes, thank you very much, you have mentioned his chest at least a dozen times—and yes, I *always* have to approve. Don't you ever forget that. You'd be completely lost without me."

I gave him a childish scowl. "Totally lost, no doubt."

Over the next twenty minutes, Dwayne sipped in silence as I recounted every tiny detail of my first full night with Carter.

I grew up in the South, and, like any self-respecting southerner, can make any one-syllable word stretch into at least three, sometimes four, without much effort. People sometimes get annoyed at how slowly my mouth moves.

Again, not *that* way, you naughty possum.

Despite my drawl, sitting at that table recounting the most magical night of my life—and yes, I actually said that—Dwayne could barely keep up. I bounded from dinner to the couch to the cuddling to the kids, then back to when he greeted me at the door in an apron. Just when he thought I was coming up for air, I went back to something Carter had said at the bar that made me laugh.

I was a babbling, bubbling, blithering, *besotted* boy.

About halfway through my endless monologue, Dwayne began grinning. He sat back against the hard, shiny cushion of the booth and cradled his coffee. Once or twice, I caught him glance up and wink. I assumed Katie was hovering nearby. I'd later learn she was eavesdropping nearly the whole time, and the two conspirators were communicating through some diner-inspired telepathic link as I talked. How rude!

Dwayne took a long sip and slowly set his mug down. I could tell by the gleam in his eyes *something* was up. He was about to spring a trap. Oh boy.

"So." He dragged the word out to a respectable four syllables. "I assume you're seeing him again?"

Not what I expected. I nodded. "He asked me for dinner Friday night, at his place again."

His brows rose slightly. "So that would be a second date, right?"

I shrugged, not sure where Inspector Gadget was headed. "I know. Hard to believe, isn't it? A week ago I was bed-hopping, now I can't wait for Friday to get here so I can see the guy I *didn't* sleep with again. Well, technically, I guess we did *sleep* together, but you know what I mean."

He rolled his eyes, then quirked his mouth into a lopsided

grin and cocked his head. I think he was trying to look innocent, like he was about to ask something out of sheer curiosity with no hidden meaning or agenda.

Now I *knew* a trap was coming.

"So, help me understand something. How can a *straight guy* go on a second date with a gay man?"

I froze, the buttery English muffin stopping just before it hit my mouth. I think I dropped it. I don't remember.

His grin smoothed, and he continued. "I think it's time you looked inward and figured some things out. If Carter really is a good guy, he deserves to date someone who has his head together, not someone scared to face who he really is."

Damn. That cut deeper than I expected.

I didn't know how to respond. My face had surely turned pale because I felt a nauseous chill all over my body. When I got the courage to look into his eyes again, he didn't flinch or move or waver. He was a rock.

I looked away.

Part of me was ashamed he even had to say that to me, but another part of me was terrified of the implications of facing his words. Deep down, I knew he was right, but I wasn't ready for that. I *couldn't* be ready. Everything I'd ever been taught— and everything I knew with certainty, everything that was good and right—told me I could never be ready to face—or admit—*that*.

If I ever admitted …

If I said it out loud …

What would my parents …

It would break their hearts.

The diner began to spin and I couldn't suck in air. I

squirmed in the booth, desperate to get comfortable, to stop the clawing heat spreading across my skin.

Then my mind flashed to Carter.

What was I doing? Was Dwayne right, was I leading him on? Was I taking a good man—*and his sons*—down a path I couldn't see to the end, whatever end that might be? Was I letting my desire to be accepted, appreciated, admired, or whatever it was I really wanted but didn't yet understand, cloud my judgment and moral compass? That stupid compass had been spinning out of control for a while. I wished it would just point in one direction so I could know what was right again. It was so much easier before, never questioning, never doubting, simply following the path laid out for me. I was beginning to wonder if my compass was faulty or actually broken.

I wanted to run from the diner, to get as far from Dwayne and his questions as I could, but my legs wouldn't move. I was stuck to the seat—and not in the fun way you're thinking of.

Dwayne's voice brought my eyes back up to his. "I need to use the restroom. Why don't you breathe a little while I'm gone? Holding it in that long can't be good for your health."

There was an undertone to his voice, but I didn't get it. There were often layers to his words, and I wasn't adept enough to see all of them, much less know what they repre-sented. His footsteps faded, but I didn't look up. My eyes were fixed on some indistinct point on the table.

A moment later, someone scooted into the booth beside me. I assumed it was Dwayne, but Katie's slender arm wrapped around my shoulders and pulled me into her. An odd mix of bacon, eggs, bleach, and cheap perfume flooded my senses. Her voice was calm as she whispered in my ear. "Sweetie, everything will be alright. *You* will be alright. You are beautiful and perfect just the way you are." She kissed the top of my head and squeezed me tighter.

My throat caught.

A jumble of emotions I couldn't name, much less understand, tumbled out of me all at once, and my shoulders heaved. I fell into her embrace, giving up any semblance of control. I couldn't stop the tears. I hadn't known they were there, but they raced forward like a horse released from its paddock, wild and uncontained, desperate to run freely. I felt them streak down my face, but also churn in my gut—and even more in my heart.

I don't remember how long we sat there, how long she held me and stroked my hair with the gentleness only mothers possess. In that moment, I needed her embrace more than I needed oxygen.

Somehow Dwayne had known that and had sent her to me. She knew it too.

Looking back, I'm sure she missed working some tables and had to get another waitress to cover, but she never looked up or fidgeted. No one ever came to interrupt the scene playing out in our booth. What an act of incredible kindness.

How had I been so lucky to have those two in my life?

Dwayne sat quietly at the counter drinking coffee and watching from a respectful distance. When my sobs subsided, Katie lifted my chin with her hand and wiped my cheeks with smooth, soft fingers. She kissed my forehead, rubbed the lipstick off with her thumb, then stood and walked back to resume her work.

I stared after her, a hollow shell, unsure if I could move, unsure if I should.

Then Dwayne appeared beside me, his hand resting on my shoulder. "Come on. Let's get out of here. I took care of breakfast."

17

———

Carter called me the next day. He said he was thinking about me and wanted to talk. Was that allowed? The Gay Handbook was silent on the point. That simple call turned me into a giddy, mindless puddle of mush. It felt amazing.

The next day, he called *again*. "Did you get my email?"

Hmm. Email? What was this mystical item of which he spoke? "Um, no. I don't think so."

"Check your AOL. I found you on there and sent you a little note." There was a proud grin in his voice.

Now, kids, some of you may be shocked to learn that the internet was not always as free and easy as the men at Connection. Sometimes, you had to work for it—again, like the men at Connection.

America Online was *the* internet service provider to the gays. Everything was still dial-up through your landline—yes, that's a phone line with wires. When you clicked the *Get Online* button, the whirring of a phone ringing would be followed by an odd series of bing-bong sounds as your computer did a virtual handshake with the AOL supercomputers somewhere in outer space. Or maybe Kansas, I wasn't sure.

There were three features to AOL that made it ripe for the gay picking.

First, a user could create a profile in which he told others basic information about himself. For most people, that included work, hobbies, hometown, and other fun facts. For gays, it *always* included height, weight, waist size, arm size, and, well, the size of other important organs. Hence, the term *AOL inches* was born, indicating someone who exaggerated the size of their, um, feet, in their profile.

The second exciting innovation brought to us by the AOL geeks was the Chat Room, a virtual place to meet like-minded people. These rooms were generally themed. One might talk gardening in a room titled *Keeping Them Green* or tennis in *Holding Court*. More adventurous men might join a group called *M4M Now!!!* Yes, the exclamation points added urgency to their, um, need. Those folks were generally impatient. I'm not sure why.

The third, and possibly most functional feature enjoyed in the AOL's magical land was email. Yes, today we take this tool for granted. It's on our phone, PC, iPad, watch—practically everywhere we turn. Back then, it was only in one place—AOL.

But there was a catch to this groundbreaking new service. They charged *by the hour*.

Stop gasping.

Yes, internet usage was *expensive*. In today's currency, you would be bankrupt, you internet-using trollop. Be thankful you live in the era of basically free interconnectivity, youngsters. We suffered for your right to unlimited online porn. Or shopping—you might like shopping. Whatever, weirdo.

Because of that last little fly in the interweb ointment, a poor twentysomething like me didn't go online very often. Yes, AOL sent CDs with hundreds, sometimes thousands, of free usage hours if you downloaded their program, but I'd long ago burned through those freebies. At that point, if I couldn't pay for it with the holy stack of laundry quarters, it probably didn't happen.

Bottom line, I hadn't checked my email in weeks, and I couldn't check it while on the phone with Carter. I needed the phone line to connect to AOL, remember?

"I need to get back to work anyway. Check your email. Can't wait to see you Friday."

My heart fluttered. He wanted to see me again. *Me!*

God, I was a dribbling mess.

As soon as the receiver hit the cradle, I ran into my bedroom, where the washing-machine-sized computer monitor blinked to life. Holy crap, Windows startup took *forever* back then. I paced for a good two minutes before the hard drive stopped spinning and I saw the happy blinky of 'you may proceed' on the screen.

I logged into AOL and the sexy voice announced, "You've got mail."

Yes, kids, that was a thing before it was a movie. Keep up here.

I clicked as fast as I could, scrolling through the spam and other emails from Nigerian princes who thought I should be their successor. About a third of the way through the stack, I found an email from Carter. It wasn't from an AOL account. It was from his *work* email.

Did people at his job know he was gay? The thought flashed through my mind, then vanished as I opened the message.

Subject: Sunday Night

Michael,

I had the best time Sunday night. I can't remember the last time I held someone all night. You didn't even squirm or turn over. It was perfect.

Bring an overnight bag Friday—but only if you want to. You don't have to. Really, it's up to you.

Work is boring today. I can't stop thinking about seeing you again.

Anyway. I sound sappy. You make me smile. Thanks for that.

See you soon.

Carter.

I lost track of time as I sat and stared at the screen in disbelief. I think I read that email twenty times. My heart was doing backflips. No one—and I really mean no one—had ever made me feel like this before. And from the bit of babble in his email, it seemed his heart was doing some gymnastics of its own.

Could this be real? Was it possible that a put-together, hot guy like Carter could actually be interested in me? I was such a mess, still figuring out life, still having no clue about most of it, and he wanted to spend time with *me*?

A sudden burst of energy sent my body hurtling toward the phone in the den. I couldn't spin the dial fast enough.

"DWAYNE! Oh my God, you're not going to believe this. He sent me an *email*. Like, a real email in my inbox to my AOL—*from his work!*"

I expected at least some enthusiasm, maybe even a show of being impressed. After all, how many people got emails?

Crickets. "Dwayne?"

"OK, I'll bite. What did it say?"

I tried to race back to the bedroom, but the scrunchy cord on the phone wouldn't stretch that far. "Crap, I can't get the phone back there. He said he's looking forward to Friday and to *bring an overnight bag.*"

There was a moment's pause. Dwayne was probably waiting for me to tell him something more earth-shattering since I'd practically declared a national emergency with my initial enthusiasm. "Alright. Is that all?"

I was stunned. How could he not see the immensity of this moment? He'd sent me *an email.* He would probably declare his undying love next. Wasn't that the progression? "Yeah, that's about it."

"Well, that's great. He's thinking about you. It's a good start."

A start? What in the actual holy gay fuck was Dwayne thinking? This was *so* much more than just a start. This was real, tangible, digitally traceable progress.

"Have you thought any more about our conversation at the diner?"

You know the sound when Ms. Pacman gets caught and dies? Yeah, I heard that, loud and clear. "Some, but Dwayne—"

"I'm glad you're excited, but you need to think about what we discussed. Trust me on this. It's important in ways you won't understand for a while, but it will make sense one day. I promise."

My heart returned from the Olympic Gymnastics Training

Center and settled back into place. It continued beating, but didn't really have its heart in it. Sorry, that was terrible.

"Can I just be happy for once, without having to think about life-shattering changes? I've never felt anything like this before, and I don't want to mess it up by being all serious."

He was quiet for a few heartbeats too long before speaking again. "Just be careful, OK. And remember—I'll be here, no matter what happens."

As we hung up the phone, those words echoed in my head. What did he mean by that? Carter and I were having dinner, possibly forking and spooning—*hopefully* forking then spooning. We liked each other. What was so dangerous about that? Why did I need an ominous warning?

What could possibly go wrong?

18

———————

It took forever, but Friday finally arrived.

The week had passed uneventfully. I worked each day, then either worked out or refereed, depending on the schedule assigned by the officiating gods. I saw Jason at the gym a few times, and I didn't trip over myself or issue so much as a single stammer when he greeted me, so I considered that flame suitably extinguished. Carter emailed every day. They weren't long, sappy love notes, just short 'I'm thinking about you' messages. Each one made my heart flutter a little more than the last.

When I opened Friday's email and saw there was an attachment, it felt like Christmas had arrived early. I was sure it was some scantily clad version of Carter with full pec exposure. I couldn't click the little paperclip fast enough, and nearly screamed as the hourglass flipped over … and over … and over. Dial-up sucked.

When the image finally finished downloading, my heart leapt into my throat.

It was a tiny, fuzzy tiger cub standing beside Batman.

Not literally. It was Cade and Christian.

The picture was dated last year, which would've made the boys two and four. They were dressed up for Halloween and ready to hunt for some cavities. Christian, the older of the two, had his arms crossed in his best 'Batman will kick your butt' stare. Cade was smiling, his grin nearly as wide as his face. It looked like Carter had caught him mid-giggle. There's nothing like a little kid's giggle. How can you not smile listening to them?

I stared at that picture for several long moments. The boys were *perfect*. Then I thought to read the actual message in the email, and my heart stopped.

M—

I forgot something. It's my weekend. Guess you'll meet them tonight.

I understand if you're not ready for this. They can be a lot.

C

When my heart started beating again, I was still frozen in my chair. I'd spent an untold amount of money remaining logged in to AOL, so I quickly logged off.

Holy fuzzy tiger, Batman.

My first thought was pure, unrepentant excitement. I was going to meet the boys. This was going to be an awesome, fun, play-filled night. We'd wrestle and race with Matchbox cars and whatever else the boys wanted to do. I loved kids. This was going to be *awesome*.

Then the angel appeared. She'd apparently taken a road trip across the country for the last month only to return hours before my moment of triumph. Her tiny arms were crossed, her tiny foot tapping feverishly—and she looked *pissed*. There was judgment in her eyes.

What do you think you're doing? she asked. *First, you keep lying to yourself about being straight. By the way, you should be straight. Being gay is wrong. It's a sin. That's clear in the book. Remember the stoning? How could you not understand stoning?*

I'm not sure which is worse, the lying or the being not-straight. We'll discuss that later.

Next, you're leading a good man down a dark path with no clear future. Now you're going to meet his beautiful, innocent children. You'll play with them and they'll become attached, hoping you'll stay in their lives. That's something you can't promise. They'll fall in love with you, with the innocence of children, and you'll crush their little hearts. You know better. You were raised *better.*

Man, she *was* pissed.

Then my bro appeared. He wasn't the devil in the red suit with the pitchfork. Nope. He was Fabio from *I Can't Believe It's Not Butter* fame, wearing tight black leather pants and *never* a shirt, just bulging, rippling muscles that poked through his lustrous blond hair as it shimmered and flowed across his chest.

OK, maybe I projected a little with my devil. It's *my* conscience, and I can make him look however I like. Give me a break.

You love kids, the devil's silky voice said. *They deserve a night of fun. You deserve it too. Don't listen to the old prude over there. Carter likes you—a lot. Trust me. I'm an angel, or I was before ... never mind. That's not important. The important thing is that you should go. Have fun. Stay the night. Get laid.*

Yeah, Fabio was right. I *did* deserve this.

The kids would know me as one of their dad's friends; the fun one, actually. They were too young to know anything else —and I was just meeting them. It's not like Carter and I were getting married or anything serious.

Yeah, thanks, Fabio. You rock with your not-butter-but-oh-so-tasty self.

Then I shook the image of Fabio rubbing butter all over himself out of my head. That was weird, even for my devil.

Decision made, I turned to pack my backpack for the night and decide which of the remaining three clean shirts I'd wear. I know what you're thinking, but it makes life simple to only have a few options. Closets full of choices are overrated.

I PULLED INTO CARTER'S DRIVEWAY WITHOUT DOING THE stalker-in-recovery circling of the block like I had on my first visit. The front door opened before I could get out of the car, and I saw Carter's tasty frame filling the screen door. He was wearing the same apron as before, this time without a shirt. Pecs poured out where the apron straps failed to contain. Damn.

He gave me a cute wave. If I hadn't known better, I would've thought he was nervous. In point of fact, I was just hoping to make it into his house without another piddle incident, especially now that I'd seen his Michelin stars peeking out from behind his apron.

As I made it halfway to the door, a tiny head poked through Carter's legs, lifting the bottom of the apron. A flash of blond hair, then a poked-out tongue, and the rascal vanished. I guessed it was a parent thing because Carter didn't seem to notice. He never even looked down.

"Are you sure you're ready for this?" he asked when I was a couple paces from the door.

I flashed him my most confident smile. "I've been looking forward to it all day."

He grinned. "So have they. That's what worries me. I get scared when they have time to plot."

I made it past the screen door and enjoyed a warm hug and cheek peck from Carter before the attack began. The same little towhead leapt from my left and attached himself to my leg. A second later, a larger version of the blond disaster darted into the room and grabbed my hand, pulling me further into the house. "Come see my room!" Cade squeaked as he tugged.

Christian just squeezed, determined not to lose his grip as I walked. I did that monster walk, stomping my foot down, just to make him giggle and squeal. That was the best sound ever.

I looked up to find Carter grinning. He started to say something, to call off the assailants, but I shook my head. "I'll go see their room. They won't rest until I do."

He nodded, his eyes brimming with *something*, then headed to the kitchen. "Yell if you start feeling outnumbered. I'll send in reinforcements," he called over his shoulder.

Thirty minutes and twenty toys later, Carter's head appeared in the doorway to the boys' room. "Anybody in here hungry?"

"No way!" Cade yelled. Christian stuck his tongue out at Carter.

"Christian, that's not nice." Carter was laughing as he said it, more amused than annoyed. He surveyed the damage. Toys once neatly housed in their crates littered the floor. There was barely room to walk. Even the bed was now basically a toy shelf.

He shook his head, smiled, and turned to me. "Hungry?"

"Yes, sir. All this playing gives a boy an appetite." I tickled Christian as I answered and was rewarded with that angelic giggle. He squirmed out of my hands and ran for the safety of his father, then looked back, annoyed I wasn't following, and flashed his tongue again.

Carter extended a hand and helped me up. "Looks like you're a hit."

"Told ya before, I do better with kids than adults most of the time."

He cocked his head, then cupped my cheek and kissed me softly on the lips. I nearly fell backward. Where had that come from? There were kids in the room!

As we walked toward the kitchen, he leaned toward me and whispered conspiratorially, "This will be a lot easier if we feed them first, *especially* Christian. We can set them up with a cartoon in the den while we eat."

And that's what we did.

It went about as smoothly as you might expect. Cade was old enough to behave, but Christian decided to put on a show for the new guy. When I sensed Carter getting frustrated—and more than a little embarrassed—I leaned over and made faces until Christian giggled again. "You'd better eat that bite or I'm gonna tickle you." I reached my fingers out and wiggled them.

He squealed and pulled his bare feet back. Carter snuck in a spoonful, then gave me an appreciative wink.

Ten minutes later, Carter and I sat around a much quieter table eating baked chicken dusted with all-purpose seasoning.

I was beginning to sense a pattern. Was this what it took to get abs? Or did Carter just really like baked chicken? Either way, it was tasty, and his abs were hot.

After dinner, the four dudes piled onto the couch. Carter sat at one end with Cade cradled next to him under his arm. I had a cushion to myself, until Christian climbed on. I watched his head swivel from Carter to me as he tried to process the scene. I would've given anything to plug into his head to hear what he was thinking. Something clicked, and he scrambled into my lap and pulled my arm around him. He wanted me to hold him tight while we watched TV.

I thought I might die right there on that couch. It would've been a *very* happy death.

I looked down at Cade, his mussed hair scattered across my shirt and bony fingers gripping and releasing my arm, as if testing if I would let go. He never looked up, but I felt the point when he relaxed and nuzzled deeper against my chest.

Carter was watching the whole time, though I hadn't looked up to notice. He reached across the couch and wiped moisture from my cheek—something else I hadn't noticed. Another simple, tender gesture to be added to the list of this evening.

My heart was full.

THE CARTOON ENDED AROUND NINE O'CLOCK AND CARTER declared it the boys' bedtime. Cade protested, but Christian didn't peep; he was already asleep in my lap.

I carefully adjusted my arms and picked him up, cradling him tightly under my chin. I almost made it to the boys' room when he shifted. Fingers brushed my chin, then traced my cheek.

I looked down to find him studying me. He smiled and said, "Mika," then closed his eyes again.

This time, when I looked at Carter, his eye was the one with moisture.

***

CARTER AND I WATCHED A RERUN OF *CHEERS* WHILE EATING our cottage cheese and fruit concoction. He wasn't kidding when he said he ate it every night before bedtime. Guess I had a new favorite snack now too.

As the credits began to roll, I turned to him and asked, "Are you sure it's OK if I stay here? I mean, what will the kids think when they wake up and find me sleeping in your room?"

He didn't hesitate. "I've never hidden anything from them, and I won't start now. They don't need to know the gory details. They wouldn't understand them at this age anyway, but they know Daddy has friends who are boys instead of girls. They'll see you as one of my friends."

I was struck by how firmly, how confidently, he answered what I thought was an awkward question. Doubt clawed at my gut, but I saw none in his eyes. He must've sensed my disquiet because he reached up and cupped my cheek, then pulled me into his arms for a tender kiss. I melted into his embrace. It's what I'd wanted all night. It was the perfect cherry on top of this cottage cheese of a day.

God, did I just say that? Shoot me now.

We kissed on the couch until the *Cheers* theme song ended and an equally familiar toilet paper jingle began.

"I can't take that tune. It'll be stuck in my head all night," Carter said, reaching for the remote. "Let's go to bed."

I hummed the toilet paper theme all the way to the bedroom. Carter finished the last two notes, then smacked my arm playfully. "I'm going to make you pay for that."

As his door clicked shut, I growled, "I was hoping you'd say that."

19

———————

I don't know what I expected, but it wasn't for the lights to go out before I'd made it two steps into Carter's bedroom. The sudden darkness startled me. Then Carter's hands crawled across the ticklish sides of my abdomen as he pulled me back against him. His warm breath caressed my neck before a sharp bite sent jolts of adrenaline down my body. As his tongue teased and teeth nibbled, his hands explored up my abs to my chest. Without warning, the gentleness of his probing ceased, and he gripped my pecs, squeezing, as he kissed my neck with vigor.

I moaned and couldn't suppress a shiver.

"I'm going to take my time with you tonight. I hope you weren't planning to sleep." His half-whisper, half-growl in my ear was followed by teeth to the nearby lobe. I'd experienced wild, passionate sex before—my two nights with Joseph and the necktie debauchery with Fly Boy could definitely be described that way—but what Carter was doing took things to a completely different level. I thought I might pass out—and we were still fully clothed.

His hand found its way to my neck. Strong fingers with well-trimmed nails crept hungrily upward. When they reached my head, they pressed firmly and kneaded, massaging muscles I hadn't known were tight. The hand worked its way up to my crown, never ceasing its caress, while lips and teeth continued taunting my ear and the tender skin below it.

I reached back with one hand and gripped his neck, pressing him into me, giving him permission to do whatever he wanted for as long as he wanted. He growled and ground his body against mine. The pulsing granite pressed against my lower back told me he understood and wanted the same.

Firm hands gripped my shoulders and he turned me to face him. He held me there, looking down, his eyes searching. Then he smiled and pressed a soft kiss to my lips, barely brushing the skin, letting me taste his tongue as it passed.

I couldn't stop the giggle that completely shattered the sensual scene.

He pulled back and quirked a brow. "What?"

"You taste like cottage cheese," I said, my giggle turning into a fit of laughter. I didn't know why that was funny, but I couldn't stop. Before I knew it, Carter had shoved me onto the bed and was tickling my sides, making me laugh even harder, this time with that bladder-squeezing, piddle-inducing glee. He was too big and strong to escape from, so I did the only thing I could think of—I tickled him back.

Nothing. Not even a flinch.

He grinned like he'd just won some undeclared contest. "Not ticklish. Nice try."

Bastard.

He tickled me harder; tears blurred my vision. Just when I thought I actually would wet his bed, his hands went from attack to entangle. He pressed the weight of his substantial frame against me, and I sank happily into the mattress as he kissed me. His tongue searched mine, as tenderness was replaced by ravenous desire. His hands gripped and squeezed, then moved and repeated. I pawed at his back, feeling the tautness of his muscles, reveling in the flare of his broad lats. Nothing got me more excited than a well-formed physique. I thought I might explode right there, before we'd even taken off our shirts—and then he corrected that error.

My T-shirt flew over my head as he ripped it off, then he bowed his head and gripped my nipple in his teeth. No one had ever done that. Stars exploded at the backs of my eyes, and my back arched completely on its own.

I moaned loudly and he stopped, chuckling. "Shh. The boys."

I turned eight shades of red. "Oops. Sorry."

He winked; then, without warning, attacked the other nipple.

Holy Mother of Batman, the Joker, and the Penguin. What was this man doing to me? How could something feel so good?

I gathered my wits enough to reach up and feel the front of his shirt, determined to do the same smooth ripping-off move he'd demonstrated a moment ago.

Crap. Buttons. Who wears shirts with buttons? Fuck me.

My fingers wouldn't work. They fumbled with the first button while his tongue wound round and round my nipple. I could barely see because every time his teeth brushed against it, my eyes involuntarily shut and my back arched again. When had I lost bodily control?

He finally realized I was never going to get a single button undone, much less remove the darn shirt, so he sat up and began unfastening them himself. That 'I won again' grin pursed his impudent little lips as he moved from the top button to the next—as slowly and deliberately as he could. With each button, I saw a little more of his hairless, rounded, hardened, perfectly massive chest.

Oh … my … sweet … Jesus.

I reached up to touch him, but he gripped my wrist and pushed it down against the bed. What was it with men and restraining my wrists?

"Oh no you don't. Not yet." His grin was infuriatingly sexy and playful.

The third button popped free, then the fourth, and fifth. Damn it. How many buttons could a shirt have? Was this thing made in Fort Knox?

He hovered over the last button, teasing me, then lifted his body and smothered my hardness with his butt cheeks, grinding back and forth with his hips as he gradually opened the last of his shirt, revealing a riverbed of stone-hard abs that made my mouth water. He was beautiful. No, he was sexy. OK, he was both.

And he was grinding. Oh Jesus.

Then he pulled his arms free of his shirt and the moonlight from the thin window above the bed painted his skin in soft light.

My breath caught. Even the audacious little angel let out a sustained "Ahhhhhh" in middle C.

Then he ground again.

He leaned down and pressed his whole body against mine, our naked chests and stomachs rubbing firmly against each other, lighting an even brighter fire in my nethers. He ground his groin against mine and I moaned again. When he kissed me, I forgot my orders to stay still and gripped his head in both hands, digging my fingers into his hair, gripping it, pulling him harder against me.

His hand reached between us and unfastened my jeans. I didn't think it was possible, but my heart raced even faster. He sat up again and trailed his tongue from the middle of my chest to my belly button, then down my happy trail. When he reached my stubborn jeans, he raised up to allow his hands to do their work. Snap; zip. He pulled the zipper flaps back and my erection flew out like some caged beast finally offered its freedom. He looked up, surprised by the lack of underwear, and gave me the most sinful grin I'd ever seen. I loved it.

He licked up my shaft slowly, reaching the rim, then stopped. I looked down to find his hands now gripping the waistband of my jeans, pulling them down past my hips. He crawled toward my feet and slowly tugged everything free.

Every move he made was deliberate and measured, his eyes rarely leaving mine, returning quickly if they did. I'd wanted him before, but now I craved his touch. I needed his warmth against my skin, his lips and tongue tangled with my own.

I watched him toss my jeans across the room with a gleam in his eyes, then stand at the foot of the bed, chest out, shoulders back. He teased the button of his slacks as he'd done with his shirt, then flicked it loose. I'd never heard a zipper's hum take *that* long, but somehow, I didn't want it to stop—until I saw what rose beneath. I definitely wanted that damn zipper to reach its end.

He shimmied out of his pants, and I saw him fully naked for the first time.

Holy Frodo, Bilbo, Sam, *and* Pip …

He was the Dark Lord's mighty tower, complete with a massive roaming eye atop its, um, head. (Yes, that was a *Lord of the Rings* reference. I'm a nerd. Get over it.) He was *huge*—and I'm not talking AOL inches either. There was no exaggerating the scale of his beast. It was monstrous and thick and … *dripping*.

My eyes must've been golf balls, because his grin turned into a full-on 'I'm going to fuck the shit out of you' stare.

My palms started to sweat as he climbed back onto the bed. His hands gripped my thighs and he did a push-up, letting his tongue tease the head of my penis. It flinched and quivered at his touch. He grinned up at me, bared his teeth, then enveloped my head between them, teasing the sensitive skin with cottage cheesy goodness. I never would've thought having another man's *teeth* on my dick would be a good thing —it sounds so painful when you say it out loud—but, as he ran the smooth tips of his incisors across the skin just below the lip of my head, and his tongue swirled around the hole, I suddenly had a new appreciation for man-teeth.

He closed his mouth over me, consuming my most precious member, then pulled back with a startled expression. He smacked his lips as if finishing a snack, then licked them. "Your pre-cum is delicious," the naughty rabbit said.

I'd never had pre-cum. Never. Ever.

My eyes flew downward and there it was, lava dribbling from the mouth of Mount Michael.

He licked it away and my whole body spasmed at the unexpected pleasure.

We spent the next eternity kissing and touching and

rubbing, learning each other's bodies and what made each of us squirm (and what tickled—darn rabbit).

I caressed his chest, licked it, nibbled it. I was obsessed. It was perfection in the flesh and I couldn't get enough of it.

He turned away and my heart skipped a beat, then he lay on his back, his erection casting a shadow in the window's moonlight. He gripped my shoulders and pulled me on top of him, then reached his arm off the side of the bed and I heard the side table drawer slide open. I knew what *that* sound meant. That's the universal gay sound of, 'Loosen that hole up, here I come.' I was suddenly a kid about to enter Disneyland for the first time. Well, I wasn't doing the entering, but you get what I mean.

Give it to me, Mickey. Come, you raunchy rodent.

Never mind. Different genre.

He squirted lube onto himself, then offered to do the same for me. I put my hand on his to keep him from doing it. "I want this for as long as you can last. The second you put that on me, it won't just be pre-cum you're licking off."

He barked a laugh, then quickly set the lube on the table. "Definitely not giving that to you for—"

He lost his voice as I raised my body and slid him inside me. He hadn't seen that coming; his eyes looked as big as the moon that was shining across my body. For once that night, the 'I won' grin was on my face.

"Michael, we shouldn't—"

I rose and fell atop him, teasing his head with the rim of my hole before taking his whole length inside me. His body rocked and his head fell backward. He didn't protest again.

I took him slowly, savoring every inch as he slid in and out, knowing we truly were one person in that moment. My hands pressed against his chest, and my dick twitched in excitement as his fingers traced my abs. Every time I pushed him deeper, he grunted or moaned. He couldn't be close or deep enough.

When I bent down and our lips met, the world fell away. All thoughts vanished. There was only the feeling of Carter and his body mingled with mine, his soul entering me, filling my essence, his warmth and passion and desire. I rode him faster, and his body responded, pushing upward with each thrust. I reached back, pulled my cheeks apart, and willed him past all limits. He struck something inside me and my eyes clouded with pleasure.

He was shaking. I was shaking.

He held that spot for a long moment, prolonging our union, then grabbed me roughly and flipped me on my back, never pulling himself free. The air flew out of my lungs as I struck the pillows, and he drove deep again, slamming past that inner barrier guarding ultimate pleasure and pain.

He gave me one last, slow, passionate kiss, then all tender sweetness fell away.

He was no longer the rational, nerdy shoe guy, he was an animal whose craving *had* to be satiated. He gripped my shoulders and pushed, using my body to brace his effort, harder, then faster. I reached behind my head and gripped the pillows as the rhythm of my ecstasy mirrored the cadence of his thrusts.

His grunts grew louder, his breathing heavy. Sweat poured from his skin, making his chest glisten in the moonlight.

I hadn't noticed him reach for the lube until his hand grabbed my shaft and rubbed slickness across it. When his slippery palm grazed my head, my chest shook, and I bit back a cry. He stroked me in time with his thrust, both becoming rougher and faster. I reached up and felt his abs as they clenched. My own responded, and my body grasped his shaft firmer with each deep dive.

He couldn't hold back. He pushed harder, and all the passion and desire he'd held exploded inside me. I could feel his cum, the warmth of his liquid, as it entered my body. I felt *him* enter me. That thought, more than any physical act, pushed me beyond all control, and I shot across his chest and abs, again and again.

I felt his cock pulsing. We shivered in unison. We didn't speak.

Still inside me, he lay atop me, smearing my cum across our sweaty bodies. Neither of us cared.

He kissed me and ran his hands through my hair. I wrapped my arms around him and held him tight.

We melted into each other, and fell asleep as one person.

20

Sunshine streamed through the window. I lay wrapped in Carter's arms, my head nuzzled in the space between his chin and collarbone. It was *the* perfect place.

Then I felt a sharp pain as a knobby knee found my gut. "Mika!" a tiny voice squawked.

My eyes creaked open to find Christian sitting atop me, his tiny hands clapping.

A heartbeat later, a second jab knocked the air out of my lungs as Cade playfully shoved his brother onto Carter and stole the spot on my stomach. He held his arms in the air, declaring victory in this battle for the top.

Carter grunted a laugh. "I don't think you need to worry about them seeing you here anymore. Looks like you've been accepted into the pack."

Lord, *another* pack. He didn't know about the wolves yet.

Cade bounced atop me and I worried Carter's other children might squirt out.

Too much? Get over it.

"Come on. We're hungry, and you have to play with us. You promised!" Cade knocked the air out of me again.

I glanced sideways at Carter, as if to say, 'Help me.'

He laughed as he tickled Christian. "You got yourself into this mess, Mr. Michael. Don't look to me for salvation."

Cade bobbed a couple more painful times and shouted, "Yay!" before leaping off the bed and racing into the kitchen. Christian, never to be left behind, threw himself down and scurried after his older brother. I watched them vanish and couldn't wipe the grin off my face.

Carter grabbed my shoulders and pulled me into him for a passionate kiss. I savored it, then pulled back.

"What?" he asked, brow raised.

"Next day cottage cheese isn't nearly as sexy." I wrinkled my nose.

He laughed and shoved me off him. "Fine. I see how you are. Can't take a little stink in the name of love."

He threw back the covers and strode into the bathroom, unfazed by his firm, perky butt smiling sideways at me the whole time.

My overactive mind was racing in a different direction though. *Love?* Where had *that* word come from?

I lay frozen in bed. Stuck was probably more accurate. The sheets were attached to my cum-dried chest. I had to peel them off, in that moment thankful for whatever act of genetic kindness had given me a mostly smooth body—the hair pull would've stung.

Carter, apparently an incorrigible morning person, raced from the bathroom and leapt on top of me, planting his lips firmly on mine. The minty taste of mouthwash seeped toward the back of my throat. "Happy now?"

"Much better, Captain Cottage Cheese."

He guffawed. "That's the *worst* nickname ever. I think you pulled it out of somewhere I discovered last night."

His finger suddenly found my hole and poked at it. If he hadn't been on top of me, I would've hit the ceiling.

I gulped back the twinge of pain and wiggled my brows. "It's the best I can do before coffee. Are you going to let me up, or do I need to pee all over your sheets?"

He kissed me again and hopped off. "I'll go feed the beasts while you wash up," he called over his shoulder as he donned a robe, then vanished down the hall.

I stared at the open doorway for a good two or three minutes. Could he get any better? Carter was hot, built, kind, smart, successful, funny, and, from everything I'd seen so far, a great dad. Did I mention *fucking amazing* in bed? Seriously. Holy crap. My butt puckered at the thought, and I realized I was sore back there. He had fucked me into soreness. Was that a thing? God, I hoped so. If not, I planned to make it one. I could deal with *that* soreness every day.

I walked back into my apartment around seven Sunday night.

Oh, don't give me *that* look.

Yes, Carter and I had dinner *Friday* night. Yes, I stayed with him overnight, then another night … then the next day. What of it? You're *so* judgey.

Speaking of judgey, Peter was eating cereal at the kitchen counter, and imagine that, wasn't wearing a shirt. My first thought was, *Huh. Carter has a better chest.*

Shit. I was smitten.

"Somebody's doing the walk of shame today," he said between crunchy bites of Froot Loops. I couldn't wait to hear how *that* healthy gem was supposed to keep his abs in check.

"Oh hey." Yeah, that's all I got out. My brain was muddled. Give me a break.

"Oh boy. He's tired. He didn't sleep much." He stood, grinning from ear to ear. "Out with it. I want details now. Start with her name."

God. "Can I shower and change first? I really need to get out of these clothes."

He hooted. "I think getting out of those clothes is what made you tired in the first place, but whatever. Wash behind your ears. There's no telling what your little tramp did back there with her tongue."

I reddened, remembering the tingle of Carter's tongue in exactly that spot, then earned an Olympic medal for speed dashing from the door to my room. The slam earned a perfect ten from the Russian judge. What can I say? Nobody loves a good bit of door slamming like a Russian.

No, I don't know what that means either. Drop it, OK?

Thirty minutes—and the longest, hottest shower ever— later, I emerged to find Shirtless Wonder still perched on a stool in the kitchen. His arms were crossed, which made his perfect pecs poke out. Why did I have to like pecs so much?

Anyway.

"Time's up. What's her name? I claim roommate preroga- tive. You have to answer and can't lie. It's the law."

I thought as quickly as I could and lied. "Pat."

"Pat?" He scrunched up his face.

Holy crap. Did I just pull a *Saturday Night Live* skit out of my ass? This wasn't going well.

Then again, the name was androgenous, could've been male or female. It wasn't *totally* a lie, was it? I shrugged off his challenge but didn't say anything, just poured a bowl of colorful sugar and topped it with milk.

I said *topped it*. Shit. Images of Carter beneath me as I straddled him flashed before me and Froot Loops scattered across the floor.

Peter's brow furrowed. "You alright?"

I knelt to gather the errant rings and hide my face from his scrutiny. "I'm fine, just tired. She didn't let me get much sleep, like you said."

He laughed. "That's my boy. Bang 'em into tomorrow."

"Oh, he did," I muttered to myself.

"What?"

Shit. "Nothing. Right. Bang 'em. I totally did. *She's* walking bowlegged today." I rubbed my sore thigh at the thought.

"'Atta boy." He laughed again. "Speaking of which, I need to get changed. It's my turn to get laid tonight while you rest your tired butt."

"*Sore* butt, more like it," I grunted, grinning.

"What?"

Crap. "Nothing."

<hr>

THE NEXT MORNING, I DROVE ACROSS TOWN TO MY DAD'S TINY office. It was attached to a gas station. Sexy, right? It was cheap, and we were a struggling family concern.

I powered on my PC and went to make coffee. Windows wouldn't be ready before I got back, so I took my time and stared at the cars as they filled up and drove away. I felt lighter today somehow. Had the sky always been that blue? It seemed deeper, richer—*bluer*—somehow. The coffee stopped perking and I inhaled deeply, savoring the scent. It was the Peruvian mountains in a mug. Wonderful.

Armed with java, I strode across the vastness that was our twenty-by-ten office and plopped down before my still-loading screen. Bill Gates really needed to make Windows faster. I was aging while the darn program powered up.

The familiar welcome tones sounded and I set my mug down, ready to tackle the day. Out of habit—yes, a habit born after meeting Carter, Oh Judgey One—I double-clicked the AOL icon. Another eternity and a dozen beep-pops later, my second favorite voice in the world said, "You've got mail."

It was nine o'clock in the morning. Was it possible Carter had already sent me an email? He'd barely made it to work himself. My pulse quickened.

There were *three* emails waiting, all from the address of the most fastidious shoe manufacturer on the planet. I grinned at the screen.

7:52 A.M.

M

I woke up smiling this morning. You did that. Thanks for a great weekend.

C

I GIGGLED AND DID A HAPPY DANCE IN MY CHAIR, COMPLETING a full revolution, which the now-stingy Russian judge only awarded a nine-point-five. Screw her and her frozen tundra.

I clicked the next one.

8:12 A.M.

I forgot to tell you, Christian asked about you this morning. He was upset he didn't get to say goodbye. When I dropped him off at his mom's place, he whispered, "Bye, Mika," in my ear.

Have a great day at work.

Tell Dad hi (chuckle).

C

SMART ASS. *TELL DAD HI.* FUNNY, FUNNY MAN.

Then cuddly Christian flooded my mind and tears threatened. That might've been the cutest, sweetest thing I'd ever heard. I wanted to grab that little guy and squeeze him, hear him giggle, feel his hand on my cheek.

How could anyone feel this way? My chest swelled as I remembered to breathe. Two full revolutions. Stuck the landing. *Perfect ten.*

Then I clicked the last email.

8:42 A.M.

Come over for dinner tonight. I know you have to referee, but I'll wait up, cottage cheese with fruit in hand.

Please don't make me wait until this weekend to see you again.

C

I DON'T REMEMBER WHAT BAD WHITE-MAN DANCE MOVES I made after I read that message. All I recall was bawling like a baby from atop the podium as the sobbing Russian judge hung the gold around my neck, and they played our national anthem.

22

The weeks rolled by quickly. Basketball season was about to kick into high gear now we were in the middle of November, and most of my nights were spent officiating preseason games or attending meetings with other stripes.

A new habit formed—I packed two bags every day. The first was my officiating roller-bag filled with uniforms, whistles, and other on-court necessities. The other was my overnight bag in case Carter asked me to stay over again.

He did. Every day.

Did you know your body could learn to crave cottage cheese? I had no idea.

I slept snugly in Carter's corded arms and woke to gentle kisses on my neck.

I didn't think I'd ever been so perpetually happy. My cheeks ached from smiling. Dwayne and I had lunch several times a week, and I grinned throughout each as he endured me recounting every detail of the prior evening's sleepover. Based on how sore my jaw was in the morning, I had slept with a broad grin too.

I needed therapy. Seriously. To all who lived through this period of syrupy sweet, perpetual bliss, I sincerely apologize.

What am I saying? I *don't* apologize. I'd never been so happy, and everyone else had to just deal with it, grin and all. So there.

By our fifth week, the L word slipped out. No, not lesbian, the *other* L word.

This time, it wasn't in the context of teasing or passionate sex. We'd just eaten breakfast, and I was leaving to drive to work. Carter raced from the bedroom, nearly slamming into a wall in his graceless socks-on-hardwood slide, just to give me a kiss goodbye. My hand was turning the knob when he said, "Have a great day. Love you."

I wasn't sure he *meant* to say it. When I turned around, his face had lost all color. Mine was suddenly covered in sweat.

I bridged the two strides between us, cupped his cheek as he so often did to mine, and said, "I love you, Carter."

He didn't hesitate. In a flash, he was squeezing me into him with all his strength, his lips glued to mine, his eyes open and blazing with complex emotion and longing.

Neither of us made it to work that day.

OUR SIXTH WEEK WAS THANKSGIVING WEEK.

Carter had promised his ex he'd take the kids to the annual family gathering in Minnesota. All of his grandparents had passed when he was young, and he was determined his boys would have that special bond with theirs. As much as I hated to see him leave without me, I couldn't argue with the logic. It was part of why I loved him.

On Wednesday afternoon, I tossed my trusty overnight bag into Betty's trunk and drove to my parents' house. My three sisters, their husbands, and about a hundred nephews and nieces would descend sometime that evening. I wanted to beat the crowd.

Don't get all excited thinking I had taken an epic road trip. They live fifteen minutes away. It takes me longer to get to the grocery store.

My mom did the mom thing, hugging me until neither of us could breathe, then chided me for not visiting more often, since we lived so close. My dad did his traditional half-hug and asked about refereeing. We worked together every day, and neither of them knew about Carter—or the G word—so there wasn't much else for him to ask about.

Pleasantries said, I went with Dad to the den, where he would, predictably, fall asleep in his ratty old La-Z-Boy while I suffered through whatever TV show he had on. No, I couldn't change the channel, that was a sure way to wake him up and deal with the 'Why'd you change the channel?' conversation. Life was too short for all that.

Besides, I was too nervous to care what was on TV.

Denise, my oldest sister, would arrive shortly with her side of the pack. Nise, as we called her, was as close to a living saint as there ever would be, at least in my book. She believed she was put on earth to be a mom, and she was determined to be that mom to as many children as possible. She had two birth children, my oldest nephews, and served as a foster mom for a local faith-based adoption agency. Over the past ten years, she'd fostered more than thirty kids in her home, four of whom she'd adopted. My folks weren't thrilled with her life choices, arguing she was stealing time from her *real children* to give to the others. Nise never flinched. She simply crossed her arms, raised a fire-kissed brow, and told my parents it was none of their business, but if they ever expected to see their *real grandchildren* again, they'd better want to see *all* of them.

God, I loved her.

Add to all that, she and her college sweetheart eloped when she was in her second year of college. I remember my parents tossing us in the over-packed Bonneville and driving hours to try to beat the 'I do' part of the ceremony so they could object when the officiant asked for feedback. We got there in time for a slice of cake.

Man, they were pissed.

Nise was a badass whose heart was bigger than all the planets and stars combined. There would be a special place in heaven for her one day, probably near the back of the dining hall by a door so she could hear another adopted baby cry. Were there baby monitors in heaven?

Anyway.

Midway through an episode of some poorly acted cop show came the roar of Nise's minivan in the driveway. I couldn't get out of the den fast enough. My dad's groggy voice trailed behind. "Hey. Where ya going? What's happening?"

I laughed. He'd be asleep again before I hit the door.

I got to the van just as the side door slid open. They had one of those fancy new minivans with doors that opened automatically. There was drama in waiting for the space-age panel to creep until it clicked.

The raucous sound of a half-dozen kids who'd been cramped in a minivan for three hours nearly knocked me off my feet. When they emerged, I actually did land on my butt.

Uncle Michael was their *favorite*. That should go without saying, but I'm happy to remind you.

Nise tumbled out the passenger-side door, all four-foot-eleven of her. For a woman who stood so tall in my eyes, she was an itty-bitty thing. It made her more adorable to me. I wrapped her in a tight hug and we stood there in the driveway until long after the kids had vanished into the house.

Of the wolf pack, Nise and I were the closest. It had been that way for as long as I could remember. Was it weird for the oldest and youngest, separated by more than seventeen years, to be the closest? I didn't know either, but we were.

"You and I need to talk," I whispered.

She squeezed me and grinned. "Let me go kiss the ring and we'll slip out before dinner."

We both refused to release our hug and waddled together into the house, giggling all the way. It warmed my soul to see her again.

An hour later, we'd freed ourselves from the burgeoning pack and escaped through the back door. It was chilly outside, so I suggested we fire up Betty and chat in the heated privacy of my *fancy Saturn*, as the family had come to call her.

After a few minutes of mindless chatter, she grabbed my hand and gave me that older sister glare that carried more meaning than any look should. "Why do I get the feeling you're nervous about something?"

My eyes fell to my lap. Suddenly my fidgeting fingers were the most interesting thing I'd ever seen.

"You know you can tell me anything."

"I know. Just give me a minute."

Out of the tops of my eyes, I saw her scrunch up her face. She did that when she was thinking hard about something—or when she was worried about one of her kids. I suspected both was at play.

"So, you know how Mom told you I was dating someone, and it was getting serious?"

Her face lit up like a freshly plugged-in Christmas tree. "Uh-huh. Her name is Pat, right?" She leaned forward and her grip became iron around my fingers.

Stop snickering. I know it was a *terrible* fake name to give people, but I had to think fast. Then I had to stick with my bad story so people didn't compare notes and figure it out. How else would I end up dating that ambiguous *Saturday Night Live* character?

"So, I have a confession, and it's kind of a big deal."

She was getting excited. Then it hit me. The sister who'd eloped was getting excited about a girl named Pat I'd gotten serious with.

Shit, this wasn't going according to plan.

Come on, dumbass. Just tell her. "So, Nise, I lied. Her name isn't Pat."

Her face scrunched again. "It's not?"

"No. It's Carter."

Silence.

She somehow scrunched her face even harder. That must've hurt. Then her eyes opened wide as recognition settled in. She covered her mouth with a hand and stared at me.

I felt that stare, physically, in my chest. It ached. The pack's religion was clear on gays. They were good as piñatas —if you threw stones outside the city walls instead of smacking them with sticks for their candy—but not much else. I wasn't worried about physical safety, but the time-honored medieval tradition of ex-communication was a very real possibility that terrified me.

The moment dragged on without her speaking—or me breathing. I closed my eyes, unable to take her glare any longer.

That's when I felt her other hand, the one that had flown to her mouth, gently rest on top of mine. I dared a peek. She wasn't scowling—that was good, right?

"Alright, Michael, I want you to listen to me. I don't want to repeat this, alright?" Her voice was steel.

Oh shit. Here it comes. Goodbye, pack. I'll miss you.

"You are my baby brother." Her voice caught. "I have loved you since the day I held you in my arms that first time. There is nothing, *and I mean nothing*, that could make me love you less. I *am* a little shocked by what you've shared, and it will take some getting used to—but it doesn't change anything. You remember our rule?"

I nodded, having no idea what rule she meant.

"Before you make any serious commitments, *I* still have to approve."

In that moment—that glorious, weight-lifting moment—I ugly-cried worse than Tammy Faye on Sunday morning. Nise wasn't much better. Within minutes, Betty's windows were fogged and we were both trying to keep our noses from running all over each other's shirts. Yeah, that part was gross.

Sweet Buttery Popcorn and Oversized Coke, I'd just told her about Carter! By extension, I guess I'd just *come out* to my big sister.

I hadn't used the G word. It would take years for my brain to command my mouth to make *that* sound. But the most important wolf in my pack now knew my biggest secret—and she hadn't turned her back on me. Or bared her teeth. Or bitten anything.

Maybe everything would be alright.

An hour later, we strolled back inside. Neither of us had noticed our mom watching from the kitchen window.

23

The following weekend, Carter had the kids again. It was unseasonably warm for the last weekend in November, and Mr. Hot Boobs decided to mow the lawn one last time before winter set in. We raked leaves for an hour, creating a massive pile as tall as Carter's six-foot-four frame, then he went to the garage to ready his super-sexy dad mobile.

OK, it was a riding lawn mower. Just go with me here.

Cade wedged himself in front of Carter so he could grip the steering wheel and pretend to drive, while Carter kept his arms safely around him in case of trouble. They began making precise rounds, creating near-artistic lines in the grass. The yard would look like Yankee Stadium by the time he finished.

Christian was left to me. We tried playing with a ball in the house, but his wild kicks nearly toppled a family heirloom, so I decided outside play might be better. After several minutes of wresting a very squirmy three-year-old, I had managed to tie his shoes and zip up his jacket, and we headed outside.

The moment I saw the leaf mountain, I knew what had to happen.

Christian was tottering a step or two ahead of me and never saw me coming. I grabbed that giggle bunny and hoisted him into the air, then raced headlong into the pile. We both vanished in a sea of orange and yellow. His squeals and giggles only swelled as I went on the attack, tickling his sides while lifting his flailing body above the leaves.

He screamed out for Carter, but the mower was too loud for his backup to hear.

I dumped him back into the mound and hopped out.

Leaves flew everywhere as scrawny arms flapped to the surface and leaf-ridden blond hair shook with glee. I scooped up leaves between my hands and dumped them onto his head.

He shrieked louder. His laugh was now uncontrollable. I felt my own howling deep in my gut.

Without thinking, I dove into the pile next to him and let him dump armful after armful on top of me. He jumped on my stomach and tried to tickle my sides like I'd done to him earlier. Tears were streaming down both our faces.

The roar of the lawnmower made me look up.

The moment froze. It was as if someone had taken a photo, snapped that moment in time, and nothing could move.

Carter held Cade tight against him, as both boys grinned from ear to ear. Cade's eyes were bugged wide as his hands gripped the steering wheel like an indie racer. My heart soared at the sight. Then I glimpsed Christian's face as he emerged from the pile, leaves sticking out of his thoroughly disheveled hair. His face held a pure, innocent joy. Our eyes met, and his smile widened, his giggles grew louder.

Click.

Each of us may have three or four perfect moments in our lives, a few more if we're truly lucky. I'll never forget that moment, that frozen instant when everything I loved and cherished—*everyone*—was smiling and laughing with reckless abandon. I can still squeeze my eyes and see Carter glancing at me out the corner of his eye, hear the laughter of a precious little boy as he tossed leaves on my head, feel the bite of the breeze, smell the mix of leaves and cut grass.

That moment will never fade.

THAT NIGHT, WE PUT THE BOYS TO BED AROUND NINE. CARTER carried Cade; I, Christian. As I laid my charge into his bed and pulled the covers snugly to his chin, he wiggled his arm out and pressed his palm to my cheek. His giant brown eyes blinked up at me, and he smiled. When I thought my heart couldn't take any more, he whispered a new word I'd never heard him speak: "Love Mika."

I gulped and managed to say, "I love you too, little man." I fled the room before my chest began to heave. I'd never shed so many happy tears. The door clicked shut and Carter wrapped me in his strong arms.

"They get me every time too." He kissed my temple. "Let's get our snack."

I couldn't help but laugh at the absurdity—and pleasure—of our nightly ritual. Cottage cheese and canned fruit. Who knew?

An hour later, we climbed into bed. Carter spooned me tight against his body. His warmth comforted me; his strength gave me peace. I felt his breathing slow and deepen as sleep overtook him. I wriggled free of his arm and turned to face him, to watch his chest rise and fall, to see his eyes zip back and forth beneath his eyelids as he dreamed. He even pursed his lips. It was cute.

It was Saturday night and my mind found its way to the Connection where we'd met. There were probably thousands of men there right now, dancing and drinking. I'd been so excited to go there each weekend. Now, I couldn't imagine going back. What was I doing there in the first place?

Then I chuckled. It was called *the Connection*. That's exactly what people were doing there; what I'd been doing there. We were looking to *connect*. Maybe some wanted to connect purely on a physical level, but I think most wanted more, whether or not they were ready to admit it.

I nuzzled my head beneath Carter's chin, just above his collarbone, and rested my hand on his chest. It was my special place, the safest place in the world. In that moment, I knew there would be no more searching.

As far as connections went, I'd found mine.

WAIT, DON'T GO YET!

If you enjoyed My Next Date, please take a moment to leave a review filled with stars. Your feedback is what keeps an independent author inspired. What can I say? We're a vain lot.

OH, ONE MORE THING

Continue with Michael's journey of discovery in My Wildest
Date. I've included a few chapters on the following pages to
give you a taste.

I know, I'm *such* a tease.

MY WILDEST DATE: CHAPTER 1

Pancake Bliss

"Just breathe between sentences, okay?" Dwayne motioned to slow the word-vomit spewing out of me. His amused grin belied his annoyed tone and motherly palm.

"Sorry," I said, not sorry at all. "I guess you had to be there. It was the most incredible day I could ever imagine."

Thanksgiving was a couple weeks ago, and perky, jingly music rang throughout the diner. I'd just talked through Dwayne's coffee, pancakes, and eggs without touching my own plate. He had practically licked his as Katie, our regular waitress, pried it from his bony fingers. They exchanged a wry glance before she shuffled off to her next table.

None of that mattered.

I walked Dwayne through the weekend with Carter and the kids, ending with a Picasso-like portrait of Saturday's lawn-mowing, leaf-pile-tossing, picture-perfect day. Carter had his older son, Cade, on his lap as they made meticulous lines in the grass with the riding mower. Carter was determined to get one last cut in before winter grabbed us by the, um, throat.

Meanwhile, I was responsible for watching three-year-old Christian. Not to be outdone by Carter's heroic ride-on-my-lap-dad-trick, I took my little monster to the man-sized pile of leaves and tossed him in. The pile shook with his giggles. Before I knew it, we were both rolling around, tossing leaves at each other, and crying with happy laughter.

That's when it happened.

I looked up from the flurry of tiny hands and fluttering leaves and time froze.

It was as if someone had pressed a button on a magical camera and everything paused.

In that moment, I had *everything* I'd ever wanted.

I had a partner who loved me, two beautiful boys whose smiles filled my soul in ways I'd never experienced, and hope for an incredible future.

Despite his palm-waving, Dwane couldn't quell my excitement.

The tiny, upturned creases around his eyes mirrored his smile, and I knew he didn't want to. He was happy for me. He was nearly twice my age, but my best friend, the one person in the world I told everything and knew I would never be judged.

Um, okay, that's not exactly true. I knew I *would* be judged. It's what we gays do, isn't it? Our DNA requires it. It's science.

Anyway.

Dwayne's judgment wasn't snarky or self-interested. It was borne of genuine empathy and concern, like a brother or father—or true friend.

"You've been dating how long now?" he asked as he eyed me over the rim of his chipped coffee mug.

"Three months."

My alarms were starting to sound. Where was he going? Was there a lesson coming from Sensei that would sober my giddy mood?

He nodded sagely. "That's a good amount of time. Just guard yourself."

"What do you mean?" I hadn't intended to sound defensive, but there it was.

"I don't want to see you hurt. That's all."

"Hurt? Why would Carter hurt me?" I *really* didn't like this conversation anymore. Maybe his judgement was judgey, after all.

Dwayne set his mug down and leaned forward. "Michael, you've barely slept a night at your own place since you met him. Things have moved so fast I can barely keep up. I know it feels wonderful right now, but Carter's life has complications. That can change things over time."

"Complications?" Now I was totally defensive.

His palms flew up in a *don't-shoot the messenger* motion.

"I'm happy for you, really. Just try to take things one day at a time, alright?"

I had no idea what he meant, but nodded as if Confucius had just granted his wisdom.

In my moment of Zen-confusion, Katie's hand found my shoulder. She leaned over and whispered into my ear, "Sweetie, don't listen to him. It's wonderful seeing you so happy."

I reached up and gave her hand a squeeze and smiled up in

thanks. Dwayne downed the last of his coffee, tossed his usually healthy tip on the table, and began scooting out of the booth.

MY WILDEST DATE: CHAPTER 2

Where Did Santa Go?

The Christmas countdown clock was ticking loudly now.

Eight days 'til Santa.

Christian and Cade couldn't talk about anything else. I'd helped Christian make his list, which consisted of more Matchbox cars, stuffed animals, and a Batman costume. Batman and Robin were his big brother's favorite cartoon characters on Saturday morning, so they were now his, too. It was cute.

Cade was two years older than my charge, which made his list twice as long. I didn't even recognize some of the toys and games on his crumpled paper. He carried it everywhere he went, as if showing more adults what he wanted would make them appear. Carter tried prying it out of his hands once, but the fit that ensued convinced us both to leave list management to the little one.

The four of us piled into Curt's SUV and searched for the perfect tree, then hauled it home and spent another hour decorating it. I'd never been into the whole Christmas-cheer thing, but the boys had won me over to Santa's side.

There's an inexplicable joy hanging tinsel with a three-year-old—and they get *so* excited as each ornament appears. His deep brown eyes widened when I handed him a plastic Rudolf, then he giggled when I flipped the hidden switch and the reindeer's nose blinked.

I looked up to find Carter lifting Cade so he could place decorations near the tree's top. Smiles plastered both their faces.

My heart felt like it would burst.

That night, during LA Law, our Thursday ritual, both of our little men fell asleep an hour before their normal bedtime, exhausted from another day preparing for Santa. Carter paused the TIVO, and we carried them into their room and tucked them snugly under their covers. I leaned down to kiss Christian's forehead and felt a tiny finger trace my jaw. His eyes never opened, but a thin smile curled his lips.

Carter was clanking dishes in the kitchen and I asusmed he was making our bedtime snack of cottage cheese and canned fruit. This was a delicacy I'd never experienced before meeting him, but now I couldn't go to sleep without it. I curled up on the couch to await my gourmet goblet of goodness.

The kitchen quieted.

I let a few minutes pass, then curiosity got the best of me, so I headed into the kitchen. Carter was sitting at the table, staring into his untouched fruit. A second bowl was made for me and sat in front of the chair opposite his.

That was odd. We always sat beside each other, not opposite—and our nighttime snack was eaten in the den while watching TV.

As I sat and waited, my Spidey sense began to tingle—and not in the good way. I knew something significant was about to happen.

"Everything okay?" I ventured.

When he looked up, I knew my world was about to change. His eyes were rimmed with red and a trickle flowed down one cheek.

"Carter, what's wrong?"

"I'm so sorry," was all he could get out before he choked on a sob. I was kneeling by his chair in a flash, one hand on his arm, the other gently rubbing his back.

"Hey, you. I'm right here. Whatever it is, we'll face it together."

That made his sobs grow.

"Her lawyer called," he muttered.

Now I was confused—and deeply concerned.

"Lawyer? Whose lawyer?"

"Jen's."

Jen was his ex-wife and the boys' mother.

My heart seized.

"Christian was so excited the other day." He sucked in a breath and locked eyes. "When I took them back to her place after their visit, he talked about it all week. Jen hadn't realized you were staying here on my weekends with the boys."

Another wave hit him, and he couldn't talk for a few minutes. I waited, having no idea what to say.

"You can't stay here anymore."

My head swam.

"It's okay. I'll just stay at my place when the boys are here. That's not a big deal."

He shook his head. "No, it's bigger than that. She's threatening to take me to court, to challenge our joint custody, if you sleep here one more night. Her lawyer said something about Tennessee judges not looking favorably on *gay influence* in situations like this."

Gay influence? What the hell was that? I understood the conservative approach to parenting—my own wolves had made sure of that—but I'd never been anything but supportive of Carter's decisions and a was positive influence on the boys. Carter and I never kissed in front of them just to make sure stories couldn't get back to mom.

"The lawyer said Cade told them about jumping on you while you were in the bed with me. He said you were naked."

"That's ridiculous." Now I was pissed. "I never got out from under the covers. The boys have never seen me less than fully clothed."

"I know, but *truth* doesn't matter, only what they can make a judge believe." His head drooped. "I can't lose them, Michael. I can't lose my boys."

His hand was shaking as he took mine and kissed it. My last defense shattered with that simple act, and I began to cry with him. He dropped from his chair and held me on the floor as we wept.

DON'T STOP NOW!

Continue with Michael's journey of discovery in My Wildest
Date.

www.ingramcontent.com/pod-product-compliance
Lightning Source LLC
Chambersburg PA
CBHW060450300726

48975CB00008B/2459